THE MOST
MAG
C

BY

FIONA LOWE

All the characters in this book have no existence outside the imagination of the author, and have no relation whatsoever to anyone bearing the same name or names. They are not even distantly inspired by any individual known or unknown to the author, and all the incidents are pure invention.

First published in Great Britain 2010
Harlequin Mills & Boon Limited,
Eton House, 18-24 Paradise Road, Richmond, Surrey TW9 1SR

ISBN: 978 0 263 87928 5

Harlequin Mills & Boon policy is to use papers that are natural, renewable and recyclable products and made from wood grown in sustainable forests. The logging and manufacturing process conform to the legal environmental regulations of the country of origin.

Printed and bound in Spain
by Litografia Rosés, S.A., Barcelona

THE MOST MAGICAL GIFT OF ALL

To Diana, with thanks for sharing her stories.

Many thanks to fellow writing mate Kate Hardy
for all her help with 'UK lingo'.

CHAPTER ONE

'BARRAGONG.' The florid bus-driver depressed the large black button on the coach's console and the door opened with a long, slow hiss. Pulling a hankie out of his pocket, he mopped his brow as the hot, midday December sun beat through the untinted windows.

Sophie Norman slung her rucksack over her shoulder and took a step down, peering out at a red sign that clearly and officially said: *bus stop*. But apart from the black-top road that stretched as far as the eye could see, straight north to her right and south to her left, there was nothing else that hinted at civilisation: no bus-shelter, no shops, no houses and certainly no hedgerows like back in Surrey. Nothing. Well, nothing if a girl didn't include shimmering heat-haze, large yellow rocks, thousands of hectares of ochre-red dirt and the most amazing jagged ranges that appeared blue one minute and purple the next.

She frowned and rubbed her forehead, trying to ease the dull ache generated by long hours of travel before it kicked into a full-blown headache. Forty-eight hours ago she'd been in Mumbai, fighting for space just to walk down the street, and now she was in the middle of nowhere. Outback Australia; nowhere. 'How can this be Barragong?'

The driver shook his head slowly as if Sophie was a bit dim and extended his meaty arm towards a smaller road. 'The town's a kilometre that way. The evening bus pulls into town, but not this one.'

'Just brilliant.' Sophie silently cursed the medical-recruitment agency who'd failed to tell her not all buses led into Barragong.

'Someone meeting you?'

She shook her head. Like so much of her life, she was fending for herself and completely on her own. Just the way she liked it. 'Due to plane delays I didn't know exactly when I was arriving and my mobile phone can't get any connection bars.'

'You need a sat phone out here.' The driver frowned at her pale skin. 'You got water and a hat?'

Sophie patted the large hiking water-bottle on the side of her rucksack. 'Always.'

'Good. It's an easy fifteen-minute walk so just stay on the road, love, and you can't miss the town.' A wicked grin split the man's jowly cheeks. 'Oh, and walk around the snakes. They'll be sunning themselves about now and they get a bit grumpy if you step on them. They quite fancy a tourist for lunch.'

Snakes? Sophie swallowed the shriek that battered her lips and somehow forced her shoulders back. Putting up with a few creepy crawlies was a small price to pay if coming to the middle of nowhere in summer meant avoiding Christmas. 'I'll be perfectly safe, then, because I'm not a tourist. I'm the locum doctor in Barragong for the next three months.'

He looked her up and down as if really seeing her for the first time. 'An English rose on the edge of the desert, eh? Good luck with that.'

An unexpected squad of butterflies suddenly collided

with the wall of her stomach. She'd come to Australia because she needed a few months in a place where stepping outside wasn't a death wish. She needed some time to live without fear, and some time to be herself and have fun. 'I've dodged bombs and rocket fire in northern Pakistan, so how hard can this be?'

He gave her a knowing smile. 'Just keep your hat on, sunshine.'

Sophie stepped off the bus. A moment later, with a diesel-infused, lung-clogging cloud of exhaust, the coach moved back onto the highway, disappearing quickly into the distance. She jammed her broad-brimmed hat onto her head and walked towards the sign that clearly and reassuringly stated, *Barragong Town Centre. Population 1019.* She smiled at the crossed-out number eight and the added nine; a baby had been born and a family wanted the world to know the news. Although given the lack of passing traffic perhaps it was a Barragong secret.

She hoisted her rucksack up high and trudged forward, glad to have hiking boots between the soles of her feet and the broiling asphalt. After the humidity of the sub-continent, the dry heat was almost invigorating, and the silence deafening: no bombs, no screams of terror, no horns, no motorbikes and no wandering cows. The only other living thing she shared with the road was a sluggish lizard with a stumpy tail and a bright-blue tongue. Slowly the blur of the heat-haze receded and the outline of low-rise buildings came into sight. She picked up her pace, keen to see the town that would give her some breathing space and be home for three months, or until the need to move on again became stronger than the desire to stay.

* * *

Mostly amiable, occasionally easy-going but always organised, Dr Jack Armitage yelled. Loudly. And with satisfying invective. 'If she's already left Adelaide and she's not here, where the hell is she? She should have been here last night and I was supposed to have left town this morning. I can't do that until the locum I arranged through you a month ago, the one you *promised* me would be here in good time, has arrived.'

He shrugged off his leather bike-jacket, dropping it onto the nurses' station in the small A&E department of Barragong and District Memorial Hospital, all the while keeping the phone pressed firmly to his ear. It took two long, deep breaths to control the urge to cut off the incompetent recruitment-officer who didn't know his elbow from his…

'Doctor, we're trying to locate Dr Norman, but we keep getting her message bank.'

Jack's jaw clenched so hard his teeth ached and he ground out the words very slowly. 'Then find out if the good doctor has even left Adelaide. Ring the station and the bus depot, contact Port Augusta, find out if she hitchhiked—but just do your job and get a doctor here or you'll lose your commission. I need a doctor yesterday because I've got an adventure to start that's already five years overdue.'

He snapped his mobile phone shut and skidded it across the desk, watching it knock into a cluster of small, plastic Christmas trees. December the first. The day the staff always started decorating; they usually had him climbing a ladder to hang the silver balls from the bright-purple tinsel. But this year this day had a huge, red ring around it on his calendar and it wasn't to remind him to decorate. It was the day he rode out of town.

He couldn't believe he was still here. The words, *just*

gotta get out of this place hummed over and over in his head. He should be gone by now. Damn it, but he'd done the right thing. Hell, he always did the right thing, and the one time he wanted to take off, deserved to take off, the bloody locum had vanished somewhere between here and Adelaide. He ploughed his hand through his hair. Weeks of careful and well-thought-out planning, weeks of organisation and working toward this point so Barragong would have contiguous medical care in his absence, had all come to this.

Even his mother had managed to leave town before him. She'd organised all her foster-care arrangements and was having a few weeks off sailing on the high-Pacific seas and yet he was still stuck here. Stuck in a town that had never really let go, a town that had hauled him back once before when he'd thought he'd got away. Now it was sucking him down and sucking him dry. He was sick of being responsible; he wanted his own life, wanted to play up, live hard and be bad—if only for a short time.

'Jack?' A surprised voice sounded behind him. 'We thought you'd already left.'

He turned around to see Diana Renaldi, the unit-nurse manager, resting a box marked 'christmas decorations' on her baby bump, and her husband Max—Barragong's CEO and Jack's good mate—following a few steps behind, carrying a ladder.

'A slight delay.' He stepped up and relieved Diana of the box and grinned. 'Still, it gives you time to change your mind, leave the man you dumped me for and run away with me.'

She laughed. 'The baby and I would overbalance the bike, and besides we never dated. You *never* date any women in this town, and if I remember correctly it was you who set Max and me up on a date.'

'Best idea he ever had.' Max put down the ladder, slipped his arm across Diana's shoulder and dropped a kiss onto her forehead.

'It was indeed.' Jack gave them a wry smile. He might not have a clue about the right woman for himself but Diana and Max suited each other perfectly. They both wanted the same things out of life—babies, a family. He didn't regret for a second that he'd set them up.

He loved his best friends dearly, but settling down wasn't for him. He'd tried it once and been badly burned, and he wasn't in a hurry to attempt it again—especially when there was a world out there with his name on it waiting to be explored. If only he could get out of Barragong.

The sound of crying made all three of them turn around. A woman in her late twenties rushed towards them, staggering under the weight of a child whose chest-heaving sobs told of his pain and distress. A bloodied gauze pad was taped rakishly on the child's forehead.

'Oh, Jack, thank goodness you're still here.' Kerry Dempsey's frantic voice matched her wide-eyed shock. 'Lochie fell out of the large gum in our front garden and he's cut his head and won't stop crying.'

Jack swallowed his sigh. He might technically be off the clock but as he couldn't leave town he might as well be busy. He was glad to hear the child's lusty sobs because a quiet child was more of a concern. Ruffling the mop of black hair on the boy's head, Jack instantly shot back in time to five years earlier, remembering how Lochie had come out screaming as the first baby he'd delivered in Barragong. He'd delivered many more since and seen them through a myriad of childhood illnesses. 'Come on then, Lochie, let's take a look at you.'

Kerry transferred the boy into Jack's arms and Lochie gave a gulping sob followed by a long, wet sniff. 'My arm hurts really bad.' The little boy was naturally splinting his right arm, keeping it pressed close to his chest.

Kerry sighed. 'David promised Lochie they'd put up the Christmas fairy-lights in the tree when he got home tonight.'

'Couldn't wait for Dad, huh?' Jack tried not to smile but Lochie had been an impulsive kid from day one, acting first and thinking much later, if at all.

Lochie nodded, his face streaked with tears and red dirt. 'I was helping.'

'I bet you were, but next time it's better to wait for Dad so you don't end up in here being patched up by me. I'll probably need to take a special picture of your arm, but right now I'm going to shine a light in your eyes.'

He enjoyed working with kids; in fact, if he was ever surveyed about what he enjoyed most about his job, he'd probably say the paediatrics component. Whether it be at work or coaching the under-nines' footy team, he'd learned it was best to give step-by-step explanations to kids—especially with Lochie, who often did the unexpected.

As Jack flicked on the pencil torch he asked Kerry, 'Did he black out at all?'

The mother shook her head. 'I don't think so because I heard his scream as he fell, and he hasn't stopped since.'

Jack checked the boy's pupils for size and their response to light. 'They're equal and reacting, so that's a good start.'

Diana handed him an HIC chart. 'If you're right

without me for a few minutes, I'll go and pull his file and start the admitting procedure.'

'Good idea.' It looked like a pretty straightforward case, and he'd handled a lot worse on his own. Jack pulled on a pair of gloves. 'Time to be brave, Loch.' He slowly eased the tape that held the gauze pad in place off the boy's forehead.

Lochie's protesting shriek bounced off the walls as the gauze pad came away and blood started to trickle down his small face and into his eyes. 'Don't do that.' His left hand came up to fight Jack's with pinching fingers.

Jack pressed the gauze back against the forehead, cursing how head wounds bled so profusely even if they were superficial. 'I'm sorry, mate, but I have to look at your head because it might need more than just a plaster.'

'No.' Lochie's foot kicked out hard, connecting directly with Jack's groin.

'Ooof.' Jack barely managed to swallow the four-letter expletive that rose to his lips as white pain shot from his groin to his hips and radiated outward with crushing intensity. With his free hand, he gripped the edge of the trolley, trying not to double over, and somehow forced a breath into stiff and winded lungs.

Lochie's wail hit a crescendo. Kerry's anguished voice tried to calm Lochie and apologise to Jack and all the while Jack's head spun with a rain of silver dots. Focus was impossible.

'Can I be of help?' The polite and softly spoken question, asked in a clear and precise English accent, broke through the chaos.

Jack raised his head and slowly the silver dots receded as his eyes merged into focus, settling on the most abundant mass of flame-red spiral curls he'd ever seen. They spilled out of a ponytail in defiant tresses, declaring themselves far too independent to be contained by a mere, inconsequential band of elastic. They tumbled down both sides of an alabaster forehead where they sat close to a pair of luminous eyes which stared straight at him. Their gaze was so clear and full of the promise of excitement and adventure, it was as if they'd thrown a lasso around him and were drawing him into their depths.

Jack felt himself sway towards her as his groin recovered fast and the first non-painful sensation since Lochie's kick surged through him. *The first pleasurable sensation to happen in months.* He jerked back, gulped in a deep breath, but the whoosh of heat tripled—deliciously so.

He knew he was staring but he was having trouble moving his gaze. He'd expected eyes of green or blue with titian hair, but instead they were the rich and seductive colour of fine Swiss milk-chocolate. Ringed with brown, thick lashes, they sat above a snub nose dusted with freckles and a mouth that curved up on one side in a lop-sided smile. Glossy-magazine pretty she wasn't but he didn't care—she'd had him with one glance of those amazing eyes.

After what seemed like forever, but was probably closer to five seconds, he moved his gaze along a fine jaw and down a smooth, white neck adorned with a heavy, silver tag which disappeared under the distinctive embroidered neckline of an Indian tunic-top. The blouse fell from narrow shoulders, pulling across round breasts. His fingers rolled into a ball as a second wave of heat tumbled through him like the roll of heavy surf, rushing the most intense, visceral craving through him, almost knocking him off his feet.

With her baggy trousers that matched her top, she looked like a nymph, a free spirit. A delectable Persephone who'd floated into the department just for him.

She's not for you at all. Until the locum arrives and your holidays really start, you're still Dr Jack Armitage, Barragong's respectable doctor and pillar of society.

He deliberately ignored the words and let his wayward gaze enjoy the way the floating material of her trousers caressed her legs, and then he zeroed in on her feet, feet that demanded nothing more than to be adorned with a delicate silver toe-ring. Instead they were encased in heavy hiking-boots. The juxtaposition startled him. Just like that, the work ethic instilled in him by his parents and his family's history saw a chance, and with moral efficiency brushed the lust away like a broom. Almost.

Jack reached for another gauze pad to staunch the flow of blood from Lochie's head while keeping his other hand firmly on Lochie's leg. He smiled politely at the visitor, and as the doctor-in-charge he said, 'This area of the hospital is for staff and patients. Please check in at Reception.'

With a sudden purposeful action, she slid her backpack off her shoulders and rested it against the wall before dropping a crushed and battered hat neatly onto the top. She then gave him an expectant smile. 'Really? The paperwork can wait. You look like you're struggling and could do with an extra pair of hands right now.' She crossed to the sink and flicked on the taps.

Struggling? Jack Armitage didn't struggle. Despite the fact that his eyes seemed fixed on the way her trousers moved across her cute behind, he managed to harness his indignation about the 'struggling' quip. 'I must insist that you leave now, Miss, um…?'

Laughing eyes smiled at him as the unknown stranger snapped on a pair of gloves with the expertise of someone in the know. 'Norman. Dr Sophie Norman. Sorry I'm late.'

Jack's mouth fell open; he couldn't hide his astonishment that this incredibly alluring woman in the free-flowing clothes was his doctor. '*You're* my missing locum?'

'Yes. It's actually been a bit of a saga getting here from Mingora via Mumbai.' Her well-enunciated words sounded very aristocratic compared with the broad Australian accent. 'Not in the least bit helped by the moron I dealt with in the agency office. But I'm here now and ready to work.'

Jack grinned at the high-class and totally sexy way she said the word, 'moron'. 'I think I know who you mean. I'm Jack.' *Not yet, you're not.* 'Dr Jack Armitage.'

'Good to meet you, Jack.'

A husky edge clung to the words as her dancing eyes brushed his entire body with a head-to-toe sweep very similar to the one he'd given her.

His blood pounded south with every caress of her gaze.

Then, like the snapping of a therapist's fingers, the hypnotic spell was broken and she raised her head and grabbed a bottle of saline. 'We'll do the introductions later, shall we?'

But it was a rhetorical question, because she'd already turned and bent down close to Lochie. With a firm voice devoid of all the come-hither huskiness, and sounding very much like a famous English nanny from literature, she said, 'Now, young man, I've just walked past some pretty scary-looking reptiles. Can you tell me the name of those scaly creatures with the blue tongue?'

Lochie's wail subsided, either out of surprise or fright, and he stared at her for a moment, completely nonplussed. 'A blue tongue.'

She nodded briskly as she cleaned the wound while Jack applied pressure so they could see the skin edges and estimate the depth. 'That's right, they have a blue tongue, but what are they called?'

'Blue tongues.'

She frowned. 'It's all right; if you don't know the name, we can look it up later.'

Lochie's bottom lip came out in a mulish line. 'That's their name. You don't know much, do you?'

Kerry gasped. 'Lochie!'

Sophie stiffened for a brief moment and then gave a strangled laughed. 'I know how to fix you up, so how about you tell me about reptiles while we make you feel better?'

As she moved to pick up more gauze, Jack caught a glimpse of grey shadows scudding through previously clear eyes before her chin tipped up and an almost reckless gleam pushed the darkness away.

It was sudden, unexpected, and it both jarred and intrigued him.

This woman intrigued him. She looked like a hippy but with Lochie she sounded very much like an uptight, bossy and organising school teacher. The odd combination fascinated him.

It's actually been a bit of a saga getting here from Mingora... The almost reckless gleam in her eyes suddenly made a lot of sense: she'd just come out of a war-ravaged area into a peaceful place. He imagined the sudden removal of the terrifying pressure that was exerted when your life was in constant danger must be as intoxicating as the finest bead in the best champagne.

And she was intoxicating. From the first time their eyes had locked her gaze had promised sheer, unadulterated fun. She had an aura of wildness about her that called to the part of him he'd locked away five years ago. The part of him that could come out and play now she was Barragong's doctor and he was just Jack. Except he was never 'just Jack' in Barragong. He had to leave town to be himself and after five years of snatched weekends here and there his time had finally arrived for a real break.

It's a shame you're leaving—the two of you could have had some fun together. Why not stay a while and see what could happen? The temptation circled him, enticing and appealing, pulling at him to break the cardinal rule he'd lived by since Mary. There was absolutely no doubt that Sophie Norman was undeniably sexy and totally gorgeous, but he didn't have fun in Barragong. He worked in Barragong. He played elsewhere, safely keeping women out of his Barragong life.

He squared his shoulders, the discipline and self-control that had kept him going for years shooting back into place. Sometimes the timing was just wrong and this was one of those times. Sophie was here to be Barragong's doctor so he could start his long-service leave, and *nothing* was stopping him from getting out of town today.

CHAPTER TWO

SOPHIE hadn't expected to meet the Barragong doctor gasping for breath just as his undisputed masculinity had taken a severe battering by a five-year-old. As she tried not to scratch the patch of stress-induced eczema she could feel had risen on her arm after treating Lochie, the thought that perhaps she wasn't the only doctor on the planet who found dealing with children difficult soothed like calamine lotion.

She also hadn't expected Dr Jack Armitage to be a bikie. Not that she had any complaints about that. Not counting one disastrous exception, she'd always been attracted to bad boys. In their uncomplicated world of no promises, she could truly relax and be herself.

And Jack radiated one-hundred-percent, dazzling 'bad boy' from the top of his inky-black hair to the jet of his leather trousers; his neat haircut jarred the image slightly, but not enough to bother her one little bit. He was a visual gift from the gods, and after her six months in a living hell she soaked him in while half-listening to his detailed explanation about clinic procedures. Procedures that were all neatly printed and stored in an absurdly organised and colour-co-ordinated folder complete with tabbed dividers. His receptionist was obviously a stationery junkie.

His mellow voice rolled around her like a caress as she followed him on a whirlwind tour. 'I usually start the day with an early hospital round before heading to the clinic, but it's your gig, Sophie, so do things your way. The staff have promised me they'll adapt.'

She was pretty sure women probably promised him anything, and why not? His large black boots connected him firmly and authoritatively with the world, and his wide, firm stance showcased strong calves and tight buttocks. The whole package was outlined in glorious detail by leather trousers that nipped in at a narrow waist. Tucked in flatly to the belted waistband was a soft white T-shirt that clung to his broad shoulders and, given the bronzed and bulging arm muscles that escaped from under the short sleeves, she imaged the rest of the shirt covered very toned abs.

Jack Armitage exuded the confidence of a man who knew what he wanted and Sophie envied him that. She knew for certain what she didn't want in her life but she wasn't at all sure she had any clue what she really did want. She lurched from one vague plan to the next. Australia had beckoned when the stress of working in a war zone had her so worn out that any loud noise made her jump, and every day had become a strategy in survival. She needed some breathing space and she needed to embrace normality. She probably should have gone to see her father but the thought of returning to England in December was unconscionable. She'd have gone just about anywhere to avoid Christmas, just like she'd done for years.

After fifteen minutes of walking and talking, Jack paused; they were now back at the admissions desk. 'So is all this making sense?' Strikingly vivid eyes—the same colour of the purple-blue mountains she'd seen in the distance when she'd hopped off the bus—sought confirmation.

Eyes that held a current of leashed energy that had sparked like electricity, pinning her to the wall, the moment she'd first locked eyes with him. Eyes that had unabashedly appraised her from across a room and were still doing it.

His gaze heated every part of her it touched, setting up an itch under all of her skin that she knew no amount of calamine lotion would soothe.

You've been out of circulation for too long and that's making you imagine this attraction. She had to be imagining it, because nothing like this had ever happened to her before and the intensity was almost scary. She breathed in a long, slow, breath; the technique she'd learned as a teenager when her life had changed forever, and then honed when working with Frontline Aid. Immediately her heart slowed down, her body drained of its heat, and she centred her thoughts firmly on what Jack was saying. 'It's all making total sense. The information's very clear and straightforward.'

'Great. Now, these are the numbers if you need to evacuate a patient.'

He reached across in front of her and grabbed a bright yellow sticky-note to mark the page; the scent of sunshine and fresh soap tickled her nostrils.

She breathed in deeply, inhaling the robust and almost decadent scent, but instead of slowing her heart rate it immediately sped it up again, overruling all attempts at calming thoughts. Delicious warmth followed a second later, building into heat which trailed through her veins with addictive sweetness, leaving hot spots of something she knew intimately but didn't want to name.

Her brain grinned, totally ignoring her, and with a loud trumpet fanfare named it: *longing.*

No. This was just the recognition of, and longing for, normality. This was the longing for a safe haven because for the last six months she'd been working abroad with the stench of war and disease in her nostrils, and she'd avoided such deep, lung-filling breaths. Now she was out in the safe desert of Australia, she could take her fill of the cleansing, pure air.

Pure lust.

Jack's head tilted sideways and concern backlit with a simmering heat flared in his eyes. 'You OK, Sophie? You look a bit dazed.'

The flat vowels sounded strange to her ears but the deep melody of his voice moved through her like the rich vibrating bass of a bassoon, before settling inside her where she hadn't known there was a space. 'I'm fine.' *No, you're not, you're wigging out. No man has ever affected you quite like this.* 'I'm just jet-lagged, with a bit of culture shock on the side.'

'England's smaller and a lot greener,' he teased, his face lighting up with that enigmatic look that sent rafts of tingling all the way down to her toes, making them curl.

She was going mad. This reaction was completely over the top for a guy she'd only met two hours ago, even if he was an enigmatic bad-boy—her type of man. Was this what happened to women who hadn't had sex in a long time? When the pressure of not knowing if you'd live another day was removed? She felt her fingers dig into her palms, trying to shock herself back into control with some physical discomfort. She'd never experienced such overwhelming need before and she was used to long periods of time between boyfriends. It came with the territory when you took contracts with Frontline Aid. Liaisons were actively discouraged because they could fracture the way the Frontline team worked, and it was enough just to stay safe and keep the nationals alive.

But living with death every day made you want to grab onto life and her body seemed to be doing that. She tucked an annoying curl of hair behind her ear and tried concentrating on geography rather than the fact that her body had totally disconnected from her brain and common sense, and was careering off the rails like a runaway train. 'True, England's small and green, but I've just come from working in north-west Pakistan, and when I was looking at its beautiful, snow-covered, jagged mountains and glacial lakes I thought I was in Switzerland.'

He raised his brows. 'Except for the mortar fire?'

She gave a tight laugh. 'Yes, well, there was a lot of that, which made it very un-Switzerland.'

He folded strong arms across his broad chest. 'I think you might find the silence of Barragong a bit unsettling.'

The concern in his eyes was unsettling. It was as if he saw way past the persona she showed the world. She much preferred the open admiration and banked heat.

She flicked the folder shut. 'Dr Armitage—'

'Jack.' The heat in his eyes flared again.

Her muscles liquefied and she clutched the folder tightly to her chest. 'I've done locum work all around the world and this—' she tapped the folder '—is the most comprehensive handover I've ever had. Between the staff and the flying doctors, not to mention the virtual consultations available with specialists in Adelaide, I'm sure Barragong and I will muddle through.'

'With your experience in the world's trouble spots, I think you'll do a lot more than muddle.'

The deep resonance of his voice cloaked her like velvet and she fought every instinct to close her eyes and lean into him. But this wasn't a smoky bar or a low-lit dance floor. This was a hospital, and she'd arrived in Barragong so he could leave.

It's such a shame he's leaving. She ignored the traitorous and tempting voice. 'So, if you can just show me where the hospital flat is, you can start your holiday.'

'Sophie, you've no idea how much I've longed to hear those words.' This time a long, lazy smile rolled across his jaw, up along his cheeks and straight to his eyes, giving him a simmering edge of raw appeal. The bad-boy appeal called to her like a siren.

Except for the dimple in one cheek. A dimple! None of her previous bad-boy boyfriends had dimples, and it certainly wasn't a look she associated with a biker.

But the thought vanished when, with one flick of his long, strong index-finger, he pulled his leather jacket off the back of a chair and swung it over his shoulder.

'The flat hasn't been lived in for years, and it's currently full of old files, so you're staying out at my house.'

A house. Delight spun through her. It had been two years since she'd lived in a house. Two years since she'd left Simon and most of her possessions, everything that had tied him to her. Since then she'd lived in tents, dorms, flats, community houses—whatever shelter had come with the job. She'd learned to travel with the basics and not unpack too much, because it made leaving easier and a lot quicker.

'After my most recent accommodation, a house sounds decadently luxurious.' *Can you hear yourself?*

Frontline really must have put her on the ropes—first her body hankering so strongly for Jack and now her brain being happy about a house. It was like being inhabited by a stranger.

Jack's smile held a tinge of a grimace. 'It's a rambling, old homestead that doesn't come close to luxurious, but then I guess it's all relative. How much gear have you got?'

She inclined her head towards her large, beloved and well-worn rucksack. 'That's it.'

The blue in his eyes deepened against the violet and his voice dropped to a low rumble. 'A woman who travels light is every man's fantasy.'

Up until now only his eyes had devoured her but this was unambiguous flirting. Her lips dried and her tongue darted out to moisten them as she met his gaze, throwing herself into the strands of attraction that had been pulling strongly between them from the moment they'd met. 'A woman who travels and doesn't stay is every man's fantasy.'

His eyes drifted over her again in his slow and all-encompassing gaze, and her breasts tingled, pushing against the lace of her bra while every other cell in her body opened up, clamouring for him. She thought she'd either ignite on the spot or melt in a puddle, consumed by need.

With an abrupt jerk, he slung her rucksack over his shoulder and strode towards the door. 'Everyone, I'm driving Sophie to my place, and as from four o'clock she's on my pager and on duty. Me? I'm outta town—first overnight stop, the Parachilna pub.'

He paused and turned back. 'Don't expect postcards, I'm going to be frantic doing nothing.'

Sophie caught a glimpse of sheer relief in his eyes

as the assembled staff gave a good-natured cheer and voices called out, "Haven't you left yet?", "Be good," "Safe travels," and "Nice work if you can get it."

Jack just laughed, turned and gave a backwards wave before he disappeared through the automatic emergency doors—a dark silhouette against the bright sun walking towards his future without a backward glance.

Sophie knew all about that.

She paused before following him, checking with Diana if she needed her back at the hospital this afternoon.

The nurse shook her head. 'Spend the afternoon getting settled at Jack's and looking around town. Mind you, that will only take you ten minutes, even if you do it leisurely. Then you can get a good night's sleep because clinic starts at eight a.m. and, believe me, we'll be working you hard on your first day.'

Busy was good. She'd learned about keeping busy from the age of twelve—it meant less time to think. 'Right. I'll be ready.'

Diana reached out and touched her gently and briefly on the arm. 'I was teasing you about the working hard. Emergencies excepted, we'll ease you into things, including teaching you about the Aussie sense of humour.'

The friendly touch surprised her. In England even when a colleague had known you for years they rarely touched you, and the women in the sub-continent had been either shy or cool. But Australians, it seemed, didn't have the same reserve. 'I'll look forward to that.'

Diana smiled. 'You better go and catch Jack or he'll leave without you, because *nothing* is going to stop him getting away by four.'

And that's probably a good thing. Jack Armitage was a temptation she wasn't certain she could withstand or wanted to withstand for very long. Still, she only had to follow him to his house, receive the key and wave him goodbye. She ignored the jab of disappointment that her body gave her and walked briskly out through the ambulance bay where the mid-afternoon heat hit her like a brick wall. The black asphalt of the car park was sticky, partially melted by the heat, and the bright, white glare of the sun made it difficult to see. She immediately shielded her eyes with her hand and squinted towards a group of four-wheel-drive vehicles all clearly marked with the Barragong Health logo. She couldn't see Jack.

A moment later the roar of an engine made her jump and she swung around to see Jack's long leather-clad legs astride a sleek silver-and-black European machine—pure motorcycle luxury. He revved the engine, flicked up his helmet visor, raised one dark brow and then winked at her.

Instantly, her legs turned to rubber and she locked her knees in an attempt to stay standing. *Stop it, stop it, stop it. So, he's gorgeous and he flirts; big deal. He's leaving town.*

And that makes him perfect for you!

Sophie puffed out an indignant breath. She'd been desperately trying to ignore the goddess of free love who'd come out to play the moment she'd laid eyes on Jack Armitage. The goddess embraced life, specialised in spur-of-the-moment decisions, and Sophie had locked her down two years ago after her life had become complicated and she'd unwittingly inflicted pain on a good man.

I'll never forgive you, Sophie. She was never going to risk hurting someone again, and since Simon she'd only dated men who were upfront about what they wanted—fun, good times and the short term. She didn't do long term—couldn't do long term—and that was why bad boys fitted the bill. It was the only safe way. But even her definition of 'short term' had never been as short as a few hours.

The engine's roar calmed to a low thrum and Jack held out a helmet. 'Have you got a jacket of some description?'

Sophie had managed to tear her gaze away from the man in black and realised her rucksack was strapped on the back of the bike. She glanced from Jack to the four-wheel-drives and back to him, confusion pounding at her. 'Are we going on this? I thought I was following you in the vehicle I'm being supplied with while I'm here.'

He nodded in agreement. 'You're being provided with a four-wheel-drive, but it's out at my place. Hop on; it's only a short fifteen-minute trip and you can cuddle up behind me if you get cold.'

The goddess beamed. *Now there's an offer you can't refuse—cuddling the gorgeous Jack before he leaves.* She almost said, 'Shh,' but somehow she managed to stay silent, probably because her mouth had dried so fast at the thought of her chest tucked up firmly against his broad muscular back that her tongue had stuck to the roof of her mouth.

She didn't trust herself. For six months she'd lived and breathed extreme caution and coming to Australia was part of her not having to second-guess every move to avoid a mine blowing her up. If she wrapped her arms around Jack, she was pretty certain she'd give into the ever-growing need to throw caution to the wind.

'Hey, Sophie, hurry up. I've got a date with my departure, so hop on.'

'Sorry, I seem to be in the habit of holding you up.'

She jammed the helmet on her head, adjusted the chin strap and reached out her hand. Her palm connected with the hard muscle of his shoulder and the tingling that shot up her arm made her stumble. Somehow, her foot found the foot-peg and with a practised swing she swung her leg up over the high touring seat, careful not to touch the exhaust pipe. A moment later her bottom hit the seat, and she no longer had an excuse to keep her hand on his shoulder, but it took a Herculean effort to pull it away.

He turned, surprise on his face. 'You've done this before?'

'A year spent in Asia and the sub-continent, and bikes are pretty much your only transport choice.'

That's not how you flirt. The goddess rolled her eyes and took over. 'And I've always been a sucker for a motorbike.'

'And the men who ride them?'

The question combined casual enquiry with overt sexuality and Jack's eyes deepened to the vivid violet of a desert sunset.

Oh, God. She'd fought her own desire from the moment she'd met him. She'd told herself she imagined his attraction to her but, despite how surreal this all felt, she knew without a shadow of a doubt he wanted her as much as she wanted him.

She swallowed hard, her resistance taking a severe battering. 'That's been known to happen too.'

He smiled, inclined his head ever so slightly and then faced forward, switching on the ignition.

The bike revved up and moved out of the parking lot. She'd handled a 125CC bike herself, but nothing prepared her for the throbbing, low, rumble of the powerful 1200CC engine that vibrated through her, building on the simmering rafts of desire that had been part of her from the moment she'd met Jack. Like a match igniting a fuse, fire raced through her, driving pure pleasure around her body and awakening it with a jolt like a shot of caffeine.

The bike sped up as it shot onto the open road. Red, black, grey, brown, green, blue and purple—the bold and tough colours of the outback flashed past in a melange. Everything was different. Colours beamed more vividly, sounds had more range and the warm desert air caressed her skin like a trail of seductive kisses. Her blood pounded faster, her thighs throbbed and her nipples pebbled as the wind pinned her flimsy top against her like a second skin. She became one with the bike, giving in to the movement, allowing the slip and tilt of the leather seat to move her forward until her inner thighs contoured snugly against Jack's legs.

It felt amazingly right.

The ever-present fear of death and destruction that had ruled her life in a war zone spiralled out of her. The goddess broke loose from her chains. *You've survived and this is your life, so live it. You know life can end in a heartbeat. He wants you and you want him. Live for the moment, because you know for certain you can't depend on tomorrow.*

Jack pulled off the asphalt at the bright-yellow forty-four-gallon drum that acted as a letterbox, remembering how he and his dad had created it as a father-son project when he was eight. As the bike bounced along the olive-tree-lined, five-hundred-metre gravel track, otherwise known as 'the drive', he grinned as he felt Sophie's arms tighten around his waist and her breasts press even more firmly against his back.

Her wild spirit had circled him from the moment he'd

laid eyes on her, but when she'd leaned up hard against him when the bike hit top speed it had streaked into him, humming through his veins. It had been a long time since a woman had wrapped her arms around him, clung to him, and he realised with a gut-churning rush how much he'd missed it.

Life in a small town didn't throw up many opportunities to meet new people nor did it lend itself to casual affairs. 'Casual' meant not being the butt of town gossip or running into the person you'd slept with one night every day at the bakery for the next thirty years. Since Mary, 'casual' was what he specialised in, and big cities were casual's domain. Each year he took a few short trips, including the four-day hedonistic party that was the Melbourne Cup Carnival, and he caught up with female friends who welcomed him with open arms, all care, no strings and certainly no spooning. The rest of the year, being Barragong's only doctor kept him firmly and responsibly in town.

This holiday was as much about being himself as it was about escaping from work.

The bike negotiated the final, bone-shuddering corrugations created by the heavy spring rain which was now a distant memory, and Sophie's arms tightened even more. All too soon they crossed the cattle grid and the rambling homestead came into sight. He entered the circular driveway and as he killed the engine Sophie dropped her arms. With a swift and practised kick, he shot out the bike stand and turned the front wheel to the left, stabilising the bike. He removed his helmet, pushed himself up and off the bike and immediately unzipped his jacket, no longer needing it.

He went to extend his hand to help Sophie off the bike and his arm stalled, followed by the rest of his body.

He felt like he was watching a slow-motion advertisement for shampoo as Sophie pulled off her helmet and shook her head, sending her thick and lustrous hair out in an arc of tight curls. Her cheeks glowed pink like an English rose, her pupils gazed at him—wide, round black discs against a back drop of sparkling Kahlua-brown irises—and her full lips parted in a broad smile. She glowed, radiating arousal like a beacon.

I've always been a sucker for a motorbike.

And the men who ride them.

Her shining eyes met his and she held out her hand. 'Now *that* was totally brilliant.'

His palm slid against hers and she gripped his hand as she slung her leg over the seat until she sat side-saddle. Then, with her hand still holding his, she slid off the bike, her feet coming to rest between his size twelves.

Some strands of her wild, untamed hair brushed his cheek and his nostrils flared, detecting a hint of sweet sandalwood mixed in with the scent of woman. The combination demolished his barely held-together restraint and for the second time in three hours he swayed towards her as if physically tugged. An all-encompassing heat tore through him, firing infernos of need like ember attacks, before draining most of his blood to his groin.

'That good, eh?' His voice sounded strangled as his brain failed to compute under the assault of eyes that told him she was on fire with the same burning need.

Her eyes darkened to the burnished honey-brown of toffee and her palms rested flat on his chest. 'More than good. I haven't felt this alive in months.'

Neither had he. Her heat burned into him. Her breath brushed his face and he saw the flutter of a pulse beating in the delectable hollow at the base of her throat. Then her eyes widened to the point where base desire conquered every other emotion—rational or otherwise—and perfectly mirrored the collision of their thoughts.

'God, you're gorgeous.'

'So are you.'

Her eyes held his and he did what he'd wanted to do from the moment he'd met her. He lowered his mouth, his lips seeking hers, and an explosion of taste met him: the spices of the exotic east, the heat and dust of the desert, feminine desire and something tantalisingly elusive that he couldn't quite pin down but reminded him of long-lost summer evenings.

What are you doing? You're leaving town.

He pulled back, stroking away a titian curl from her cheek, only to have it wind itself around his finger like a clinging vine. 'I'm sorry, I shouldn't have done that. This timing totally sucks, because you're absolutely dazzling but I'm leaving today for a minimum of three months.'

Her clear gaze didn't waver, nor did it look offended. 'And would you have pulled away from the kiss if you weren't leaving?'

He shook his head. 'Hell, no.'

She smiled. 'So you would have kept kissing me, and then what?'

He hadn't expected that question but then again he'd never met a woman quite like her. 'Are you asking me what my intentions were?'

Her hands rested gently on his chest. 'Would you have wined and dined me before inviting me into your bed?'

He prided himself on the way he entertained women. 'Of course I would. But after the meal I'd have shown you the glory of the outback night sky, devoid of rocket fire, and then introduced you to the southern constellations and the Southern Cross.'

She sighed. 'No sounds or sights of war. That sounds brilliant. And then? Would we spend a few weeks having fun before we both parted amicably?'

He blinked at her refreshing candour. 'Fun sounds perfect, because I'm not looking for anything permanent.'

The shadows scudded past, dark against her milk-chocolate eyes. 'Neither am I.'

He groaned at the way the universe was thumbing its nose at him. The perfect woman who didn't want a long-term relationship and only wanted fun had just walked into his life, and he was leaving. Every part of him wanted her and every part of her seemed to be vibrating the same message back at him.

Even if you weren't leaving you're still in Barragong. He ran his hand through his hair. 'This is insane. We've just met but this thing between us, it's—'

'Like a force field.' She bit her lip and blinked before raising her eyes to his, the dusky traces of shadows hovering. 'I've never done anything like this before in my life either, but I've just walked out of a horrendous half year where I've seen more horror than anyone should witness, and I know *nothing* is permanent. Tomorrow may never come.'

He needed her to understand. 'I can't promise you anything, Sophie.'

'I don't want or need promises—my life doesn't work that way.' Her fingers traced across his chest. 'Sometimes we just have to take the good things when they come. I've just come out of a war zone, you're leaving on a much-needed holiday and perhaps this thing between us exists so strongly because we both need it. Maybe we each have what the other needs right now, just for today.'

His body craved hers like the sun-parched desert craved water. 'Are you totally certain about this? I don't want to hurt you, Sophie.'

Faint lines appeared on her forehead. 'I don't want to hurt you either.'

He'd never felt so torn. 'I'm leaving in an hour.' *Shut up, Dr Jack.*

Her hand cupped his jaw. 'I know you are and that gives us plenty of time. Consider me your first "holiday treat".'

The word 'holiday' banished Dr Jack and released Jack the man. He circled her waist with his hands, pulling her hard against him. 'In that case, consider me your Barragong welcome-basket.'

She tilted her head back, hooking his burning gaze with one of her own. 'That works for me, Jack.'

It was all he needed to hear.

His lips sought hers again, his mouth playing over the lush softness of her lips, his fingers dragging through the thick tangles of her hair, liberating the aroma of tangerine and more sandalwood. He inhaled deeply, revelling in the way the scent released a sense of freedom in him he'd never known.

He heard himself sigh and then her mouth opened under his, inviting him in, hauling him in as her tongue met his with the same eager strokes that he was using. He devoured her touch, her taste, her scent, the blissful sounds from her throat, completely oblivious to the heat of the sun until the harsh screech of a flock of birds flying overhead startled her, and she abruptly broke the kiss, her head turning sharply.

'What was that?' The words tumbled from the sexiest mouth he'd ever encountered.

'Galahs. Get used to the sound, because they'll wake you at dawn.' He swung her into his arms and, taking two steps at a time, bounded up to the front door. 'Time to bring this inside. I've no plans to compete with what to you is exotic wildlife.'

As they passed through into the hall, she swung an arm around his neck, her fingers massaging the back of his head. 'So you can't do wild?'

His groin ached and his hands tightened around her as he kicked opened his bedroom door. 'Sweetheart, I can do whatever you want me to.'

She laughed, a sound of pure delight, as he dropped her gently onto his bed. Her hand reached out and clasped around the waistband of his trousers, pulling him forward. 'I'll hold you to that.'

Keeping his gaze fixed firmly on her eyes, eyes bright with thundering need, he leaned sideways and reached into a drawer, hoping a stray prophylactic was there because it had been a very long time since he'd had sex in this bed. He almost laughed with relief when his fingers gripped the familiar square foil and he held it up like a well-earned trophy. With the roar of pure, base, untainted lust in his veins he joined her on the bed and opened himself up to the unparalleled ecstasy of holiday sex—casual, no spooning and no strings attached.

CHAPTER THREE

SOPHIE dreamed her cheek was being brushed by fine black stubble and soft lips. A blissful sigh rolled through her as she gave herself up to the deepening dream and let it take her to a place filled with a tranquillity and joy unlike anywhere she'd ever known. The scream of rocket fire shattered the serenity and she sat up fast, sweat beading on her brow and her hand tightly clutching the sheet.

Adrenaline jetted through her, and she frantically glanced around, looking for safety. Double bed, large polished-redwood wardrobe, a wicker laundry-basket and her old blue rucksack. Her brain engaged, her held breath released in a whoosh and everything fell into place.

Jack's room. Jack's house. The roar wasn't rocket fire at all—just the sound of his motorcycle engine's ignition and fast acceleration. Jack had just left on his holiday.

She fell back onto silky-soft, high-thread-count cotton sheets and sprawled out across the bed just because she could, loving the luxury of having a queen-size bed to herself after the narrow confines of camp beds. She breathed in deeply and the fragrance of Jack rushed through her, making her thighs tingle just like he had, and then some.

The sheets smelled of Jack, her pillow smelled of Jack and she grinned, remembering how he'd generously treated her to a smorgasbord of himself, making sure she was completely replete before he left. Wild, sexy and with a mouth that had touched parts of her that had grown dusty from lack of use, she didn't regret for one minute letting the goddess loose again and running with the bad boy.

'Bad' was all she allowed herself these days and Jack Armitage was deliciously bad.

A memory of Simon surfaced, all anguished eyes and barely contained fury. She shut it out and focussed on Jack. He'd left as promised, gone from her life as planned, which was perfect because, although it had been the best sex she could remember, that was all it was: sex, fun and no looking back. Jack wouldn't be blaming her for breaking his heart and ruining his life, in fact he wouldn't even be thinking of her full stop. All he'd be thinking of was the open road.

That's what you wanted, right?

She rolled over and caught the time. Four o'clock. She closed her eyes with a groan and then opened them again. She really needed to get up because if she slept now she'd be awake at three a.m. It was bad enough having to do that on-call, so it was completely crazy to do it if there was no reason. Fighting the tendrils of fatigue, she swung her legs out until her feet touched bare polished boards, the cool feel of them reminding her she had a house to explore, her home for the next three months.

Apart from Jack's room, all she'd seen of the house was what she'd noticed when they'd pulled up on the bike and that had been pretty impressive. Made of what she assumed was the local stone—a combination of cream, rust-red and deep yellows— it had an enormous veranda around at least three sides and it said, 'old, large and full of stories'. It didn't remotely say, 'bachelor pad'.

She padded towards a door and stepped into an *en suite* bathroom. It was like being in a hotel, with its basket of rolled fluffy-soft towels and a range of soaps, and a far cry from her Frontline accommodation. After a quick shower she was soon stepping into a pair of crumpled shorts and an old T-shirt and crossing Jack's room to enter the hall.

With a wide, central corridor, deep skirting-boards, high ceilings and numerous doors opening off from the hall, the old homestead reminded her of the only house of her childhood she had ever bothered to remember: the house in Surrey where life had been happy and the family had all been together. The place where they'd celebrated their last Christmas before their lives had changed irreparably and the fabric of their family had been cruelly ripped apart.

She started opening doors and found a sitting room with a well-worn but comfy-looking couch, two winged chairs with matching ottomans, a large-screen television and the biggest DVD collection she'd ever seen. It said, 'home; retreat from the world' and Sophie smiled in anticipation of catching up on years of missed films. The next room contrasted so dramatically with the sitting room that she gasped. In the centre of a large room with floor-to-ceiling windows which opened onto the veranda was an enormous mahogany dining table complete with sixteen chairs. Two brightly gleaming silver candelabra sat on a large sideboard, hinting at a full set of china and cutlery tucked away behind its carved doors. She felt her brows draw together. Somehow she couldn't quite match the image of Jack the biker-doctor with the elegant style of entertaining this room absolutely demanded.

Two doors remained before the house opened up into a modern kitchen and living area and she crossed the hall to investigate. The china door-handle felt cool to her touch as she turned it and the door swung open to reveal a bedroom that obviously belonged to an older woman. Floral curtains pulled back with a tasselled tie let sunshine spill in over an intricately quilted white bedspread tucked in around an iron bed-end. A massive wardrobe took up one wall, a light-cotton cardigan was draped over the back of a chair and a beautifully carved dressing-table held a large silver photo-frame containing a black-and-white photo.

Sophie picked it up, and suddenly Jack's eyes reflected straight back at her, only the face wasn't Jack's. She was pretty certain she was staring down at Jack's father when he had been much the same age as Jack was now. She set down the photo and turned to examine the plethora of other photo frames of various shapes and sizes that adorned a tallboy. All the photos were of people—a child sitting on Santa's lap with last year's date clearly above Santa's head, another child on a horse, children playing in a pool—but it was the picture of a family group that really caught her eye. A woman stood surrounded by three younger adults—two women and Jack. Was this Jack's mother's room? Were these children her grandchildren?

Suddenly feeling like she was prying, she backed out of the room, closing the door firmly behind her, and she opened the final door. She blinked at the bright-pink room with its pink-and-blue-striped curtains. Stuffed toys tumbled out of a box and books and puzzles mixed chaotically on shelves, having been put away haphazardly. It was without doubt a little girl's room, but it didn't have the faded, aged look of a room once used, loved, and now abandoned. Nor did it have the feel of a space kept as a memorial, forever trapping the memory of a child the age they had been the last time they'd used the room. Sophie could recognise rooms like that in a heartbeat. No; this room lived in the here and now, its tale told by the presence on the window sill of the current fad doll-craze sweeping the western world. Perhaps it belonged to one of the children in the photo. Jack's niece, perhaps?

Jack's daughter? Why else would a man live with his mother?

Does it matter and do you really care?

She gave herself a shake. No, none of it mattered. All that mattered was this was her house for her exclusive use over the next three months, the perfect place to avoid Christmas. She pulled the door shut with a click and decided she needed a cup of tea before she did any more exploring and found a bedroom for herself. A cup of tea, a biscuit and then she'd make a shopping list for her supply-trip into town. *A shopping list.* She laughed out loud, recognising the irony. She'd never been one for domesticity, not since she'd been seventeen anyway, but there was something about this house that made her want to try.

The kitchen was at the end of a large sunroom and it combined farmhouse cosiness with modern practicality. While she waited for the stainless-steel kettle to boil, she picked up a worn, leather book with faded tooled-gold writing. Running her fingers over the indentations, she traced the word 'guestbook' before opening the cover:

Welcome to Armitage Homestead, built 1885.
Please sign our guestbook.

Armitage. The name hit her in the chest. Jack's surname. Had Jack's family been in this region and lived in this house for over a hundred and twenty years? The thought utterly boggled her mind, because her own family had moved often and she'd moved even more. She scanned the entries of the last thirty years and imagined all sorts of dignitaries sitting around that very impressive table. Jack had called this place a rambling homestead, and he was right, but that didn't lessen the fact that this house was steeped in history. His family's history. A history that connected him to this house and this town. The concept of belonging like that was completely alien to her.

As she sipped her tea, she noticed a black folder on the flecked-granite bench and she pulled it towards her. It was filled with detailed information about the house such as where the keys to the car were hung and where cleaning supplies were kept and it included many instruction pamphlets, all filed alphabetically, detailing how all the appliances worked. It had all the same dividers in it as the procedure folder Jack had given her at the hospital, the one she'd assumed his receptionist must have put together.

She wrinkled her nose. She guessed he could have beamed his flirting smile and convinced his receptionist to make up this folder as well. A flash of the serious-eyed doctor giving orientation suddenly jumped unbidden into her brain, lingering for a moment before being quickly replaced by the image of the man in leather, which was how she'd always remember her welcome gift to Barragong. But the delicious welcome was sadly over and now it was time to focus on being Barragong's doctor.

Jack had left maps and a GPS so she studied the route back into town and found shopping bags in the large walk-in pantry that groaned with food. She could probably live off the contents for the full three months and restock at the end of her contract, but she never depended on anyone. She'd see to herself, starting from today. Glancing at the house map in what she'd christened 'the useful OCD folder', she located the office and in it, pen and paper to make her list. A sticky note was stuck to the computer screen: 'Use the internet. Password in instruction folder'.

She shook her head, a silent chuckle on her lips. Of course it would be.

'Min! I'm here.'

An excited child's voice accompanied by the echoing sound of fast-running feet on the bare boards made Sophie jump and duck under the desk. Her hand flew to her chest as her heart hammered fast against her ribs, and she breathed deeply to find calm before investigating.

'Min, are you hiding?' The voice had gone from excited to confused.

Sophie returned to the sun room to find a dark-haired little girl standing in the middle of the room wearing grubby yellow shorts, a faded and too-small T-shirt and with a pink, plastic rucksack on her back. She clutched a soft-toy emu firmly in the crook of her elbow, its legs dangling against her tummy, its body squished against hers and the vivid-blue neck leaning rakishly over her arm. The beady eyes, astonishingly similar to the live version of the bird, bored into Sophie, making her shiver. The intense brown eyes of the child had the same effect.

'Who are you?' The little girl stared straight at her with the open scrutiny of a child.

The patch of eczema on Sophie's arm prickled and itched. 'I'm Sophie.'

The child frowned. 'Where's Min?'

'I'm sorry, I don't know who Min is.' She tugged at a damned curl that fell over her eyes. 'Where did you come from?'

'You talk funny.'

Sophie sighed, trying to keep a lid on the rising anxiety she always experienced when dealing with children. 'Yes, well, that's because I'm from England. Where's your mother?'

The child pointed behind her, back towards the front door, as she ran past Sophie towards the back wing of the house calling out, "Min."

Sophie hesitated for a moment, trying to decide if she should follow the girl and tell her no one else was here or to go and find her mother. A second later she jogged up the hall, astonished to find the front door wide open. She stepped onto the veranda, expecting to see a woman waiting for an invitation to enter, but apart from the cane chairs the veranda was empty. A low-slung, rusted station-wagon, packed to the gunnels and with a plume of red dust trailing out behind it, was on the opposite side of the circular drive, heading away from the house and back towards the cattle grid.

With a shout, Sophie leapt off the top step of the veranda and hit the ground running, waving at the car. A woman hung her head out of the window, nodding, and waved back. Sophie stopped running and breathed out before catching her breath, fully expecting the car to reverse back to her. It didn't. It just kept moving forward and in a heartbeat it had crossed the grid with a loud thrum and disappeared around the bend and out of sight.

Stunned disbelief rocked her to her toes. The mother of the child in the house had just driven off, leaving her daughter without so much as a 'by your leave'. It was incomprehensible. Exactly what sort of country was Australia if children were just dumped? Her brain struggled to make sense of it all. Who was the child and who in heaven's name was Min? But, most of all, how on earth was she going to deal with a little girl?

Sophie forced herself to head back inside, a million questions pounding her, and she found the little girl in the pink bedroom, sitting on the floor looking at a book. She still clutched the toy emu tightly but the rucksack had been abandoned on the floor.

Sophie stood in the doorway, wondering what to do and say next. 'Is this your room?'

The child's little shoulders rose and fell. 'When I come and see Min.'

Sophie's eczema burned with an insatiable itch. 'But Min's not here.' She heard the slight rise of hysteria in her voice and tried to pull in deep, calm breaths, the ones that had kept her in control in a war zone. This wasn't a war zone but it held its own terrors.

I hate you, Sophie, I really hate you.

She pressed her fingers to her now-throbbing temples. This situation was insane; she was quizzing an unreliable pre-schooler for information but she didn't have much of a choice. Who dropped their child at a house without making sure there was an adult at home?

She stepped into the room and immediately felt like

a giant, so she sat down on the floor. 'You know I'm Sophie, so what's your name?'

The child looked at her with enormous chocolate eyes. 'Imogen.'

'Imogen, do you know Dr Jack?' The words snapped out in the brisk tone that always surfaced when she was nervous and she held her breath, wondering if the child would answer.

The girl nodded. 'His room's over there. She pointed vaguely towards the door and giggled. 'We dance to the Wiggles.'

Sophie's crowded brain saw Imogen point in the correct direction. If Imogen knew that was Jack's room, then she knew the layout of the homestead. 'Can you show me Min's room?'

''Course I can.'

They both stood up and Sophie followed her to the bedroom next door, the room with all the photos. 'So this is Min's room, is it? Can you show me Min in a picture?' Sophie pointed to all the pictures on the tallboy.

'Can't see.' Imogen dropped the emu and turned around with her arms outstretched. 'Lift me up.'

'All right.' Sophie licked her lips and moved to stand behind the child. Placing her hands around Imogen's waist, she picked her up and held her out in front of her like a package.

'That's Min.' The child pointed to the family group photo. 'Ouch, you're hurting me.' She wriggled and kicked her feet out against Sophie's legs.

'Sorry.' Sophie almost dropped her in her haste to put her down and then picked the photo up off the tallboy and squatted down so she was at the same height as Imogen. 'So, which one is Min?'

A pudgy finger pointed to the older woman who stood

with matriarchal dominance in the centre of the group. The woman with Jack's mouth and nose—the woman Sophie would bet money on was Jack's mother.

'Min's my special gran.'

So Jack's mother was her grandmother. 'And which one of these ladies is your mother?'

Imogen shook her head.

Sophie sought confirmation. 'None of these ladies are your mother?'

'No.' Imogen shook her head firmly. 'Min is them's mum.'

'Min is *their mother*,' Sophie automatically corrected as she stood up and put the photo back in place, her head spinning. *Min's my special gran.* Imogen's knowledge of the family tree, her raven hair so close to the colour of Jack's… Was this Jack's daughter?

No! Jack wouldn't leave a child without care.

Why not? You know nothing about him except he had sex with you and has ridden out of town on his bike. This child could be the result of a similar fling.

Seeds of doubt rumbled inside her, just waiting for a drop of incriminating water so they could sprout.

Sophie scratched her inner elbow. Hard. *Focus on the child.* She had a little girl in the house and no idea where the elusive Min was; no idea where Jack was.

Breathe and think. Surely there was something in the folder, a contact number? She wracked her brains trying to remember what Jack had said to the staff when he was leaving the hospital. *First overnight stop, the Parachilna pub.*

She pulled out the map, turned on the GPS and located the dot on the map that was Parachilna. Perhaps she should ring Diana first?

'When's Min coming home?' Imogen's thumb crept

to her mouth as she picked up the emu and cuddled it tightly.

I wish I knew. 'Let's go and find out, shall we?'

Jack leaned against the long, wooden bar at the Parachilna pub, sinking his first ice-cold beer and revelling in the live music from one of South Australia's best blues bands. Later in the evening they'd play in the old shearing shed to an eclectic crowd ranging from locals, to Sydney executives, to a noisy group of backpackers from all over Europe. Parachilna was barely a dot on the map but the pub was known worldwide for its 'feral food' and outback hospitality. As a nod to the looming festive season, the bar had a couple of tubs of eucalypt saplings, their thin branches weighed down by Christmas baubles.

A group of six tall, willowy blonde women Jack guessed were from Scandinavia kept laughing and tossing their hair and sending him fairly pointed glances. He was now officially on holidays—out of Barragong and well on his way. The invitation to flirt with a group of pretty young women should have had him pulling up a chair and regaling them with tall tales of the outback, but he had no interest in being a raconteur tonight. He smiled before turning away to chat to the bar tender, and for the hundredth time since leaving home and making the two-hour journey to Parachilna he thought of Sophie, the woman he was supposed to have left firmly behind in Barragong.

He'd never experienced such an intense attraction for any woman before, not even Mary. It was as though he'd been hurled towards Sophie by an unstoppable gravitational force. She'd given herself to him with an almost untamed passion, a ferocity of pleasure that had initially stunned him but had then entered his own veins and urged him on to do the same. 'Amazing sex' didn't come close to describing it.

Consider me your first holiday treat. He heard her high-class accent, so at odds with the other wonderful things her mouth could say and do, and he laughed out loud. She'd kick-started his holiday with a huge bang and he was finally on his way. So what the hell was he doing thinking about a woman in the town he'd worked so hard to actually escape? He had three months ahead of him where he didn't have to think about Barragong at all.

The band took a break and he pushed his glass towards Greg, the barman. 'Another, thanks.' He glanced back at the young women and one of them waved.

Greg filled a clean glass with the cold amber fluid. 'Do you want to order dinner now before the rush?'

'Good idea. I'll have the blackened kangaroo-fillet with corn-coriander salsa.'

'Good choice. I'll bring it over to you at that table over there, shall I?' He inclined his head towards the Scandinavian beauties.

Holidays mean doing whatever you want, whenever you want. No rules. 'Why not?' Jack picked up his beer and slid off the bar stool, making his way over to the table.

As he neared, the conversational buzz of the bar suddenly dropped to a low hum and the women's eyes looked beyond him. Wondering what or who had caught their attention, he started to turn when he heard, "Excuse me?"

Two words spoken in the brisk accent of a British nanny silenced the bar completely. 'Is Dr Jack Armitage here?'

Sophie. He'd recognise those clipped vowels anywhere. A rush of desire rocked through him. But, as he spun around, unease instantly returned his blood to his head, along with rational thought and a barrage of questions. Sophie belonged in Barragong, being the town's doctor. She did *not* belong here on his holiday. He pushed forward through the crowd.

Sophie stood in the doorway, her red hair now flaming as the tight curls captured the glint of the early-evening sun reflecting off the ochre soil. Her soft cheeks had an unfamiliar hard edge and her melt-in-your-mouth, milk-chocolate eyes, which had radiated lust and pleasure, now glinted with confusion and determination.

'Jack!'

Time wound down to incremental flashes—a child's voice, Sophie's arm being jerked forward before falling back by her side, a dash of movement across the floor followed by a thump against his legs. Surprise made him look down; a small black-haired head rested against his thighs. 'Immy?' His hand automatically caressed her hair in a loving gesture as his thoughts scrambled to find purchase.

Imogen belonged in Barragong.

Sophie belonged in Barragong.

He glanced to Sophie, taking in her reproving gaze, before returning to Im's upturned face that held the needy and yet resigned look of a child desperate for love and trying hard to find it.

A child his mother supported with respite care when Imogen's mother couldn't cope or didn't want to even try.

A child needing to be cared for. Today. Right now.

And his mother was in the Pacific, weeks away from Barragong.

A bolt of iridescent white fury thundered though him. *Why now, Kylie?* But the question was rhetorical, because the answer wouldn't change a thing. A little girl needed caring for and he had to find someone to do it. The iron bars of duty clanged loudly as they crashed into place, encasing him like a jail. Barragong had done it again. His long-anticipated holiday had just been seriously derailed but, if he had anything to do with it, it wouldn't be for very long.

CHAPTER FOUR

'SOMEBODY told me there is a doctor here?' A German backpacker arrived, panting, at the door. 'My girlfriend, she is feeling sick for all of the day. Can you come to her in the hostel?'

Jack picked up Imogen, hitching her to his hip. 'Sure, mate, just give us a minute, OK?' He needed to hear the story behind Sophie's unexpected arrival with Imogen, even though most of him knew it was probably one-hundred-percent to do with the unreliable Kylie and sadly nothing to do with Im's father, who'd shot through years ago.

But the backpacker instead turned to Sophie, his voice suddenly breaking with emotion. 'Please, she is very sick.'

Sophie nodded. 'I'll come now. Just let me get my bag from the truck.' She stepped out from under the veranda and marched towards the four-wheel-drive, the gravel crunching loudly under her boots.

'Soph.' Jack called out to her but Sophie just kept walking, the set of her shoulders clearly saying, *I'm busy, don't mess with me.* Well, it was too late for that; he'd messed plenty, but the fact they'd had sex was irrelevant. He wanted answers about Imogen. He strode out and caught her up. 'Surely we can walk and talk?'

Her eyes flashed. 'Not in front of—'

'Please can you hurry?' The German backpacker urged Sophie on.

'Are you a bloody Australian, Jack?' Imogen asked, pressing in against his shoulder.

He gave a wry smile, the words going some way to denting his fury with Kylie and the world, reducing it all to a dull roar. 'Is that what Sophie called me?'

'I thought you were asleep!' Sophie sounded aghast as she reached the vehicle.

The little girl shrugged as if it was no big deal, which for Im it wouldn't be. Sadly, she would have heard a lot worse. 'She said it in the car when we left home and when the kangaroo jumped on the road. She talks funny.'

Jack nodded, although 'funny' wasn't the word that came to mind. *Sexy.*

Let it go, mate. One night only.

Sophie hauled out the medical backpack followed by a bright-pink backpack and Im's tatty but much-loved Sheils, the emu. She pushed the child's belongings into his chest. 'Here are your things, Imogen. It was nice to meet you, but I have to go and help someone now, and Jack will look after you.' She shot him a pointed look and walked away with the young German.

Nice to meet you? He shook his head in disbelief. It was like she was talking to an adult, not a five-year-old girl. Jack watched her go, tamping down his frustration, even though he knew Sophie was right. The patient came first and he couldn't really talk to her with Imogen present. He sighed, a long, resigned breath. He'd just have to wait.

He readjusted the little girl onto his hip. The poor kid had black rings under her eyes and looked exhausted, but that was too often the case when her mother was busy chasing the next unobtainable dream rather than looking after the needs of her child. 'Are you hungry, Im?'

'No.' Her head dropped to his shoulder and her thumb crept to her mouth.

He stroked her hair, tucking her head into his neck. The kid needed a bed and a decent sleep. He headed back to the hotel but bypassed the bar and instead walked to his room. Pulling back the sheets, he lowered Imogen into the bed. 'Now, you and Sheils cuddle up, OK, and have a sleep. When you wake up someone will be here. Me or—'

'Min?'

'Sorry, sweetheart, but Min's not here. She's on a big ship, having a holiday.' He could string Kylie up for doing this to Im.

Her lids drooped. 'Sophie?'

'Probably not Sophie. Another grown-up, but I won't be far away, I promise.'

Most kids would have kicked up a fuss. Not Im. She just accepted what he said, closed her eyes and snuggled down. Jack's heart bled that she was so accommodating and that her life was so chaotic. He leaned forward and brushed her forehead with his lips, feeling like he'd been split into two distinct parts that never met—absolute rage towards her unreliable mother and a deep caring for this little girl with a tough life.

He left a lamp on low and crossed the room to the bathroom. Stripping out of his leathers, he took a shower, letting the warm water stream over his body, removing the traces of the man who'd left Barragong on a motorbike. He rubbed himself dry as the last vestiges of 'holiday Jack' got locked down, and he pulled on clean clothes. He rang Reception and one of the young women who'd checked him in promptly offered to sit with Imogen for an hour, giving him some time to find a way through this kerfuffle.

Sophie bit her lip and re-examined the feverish young woman with heavy-lidded eyes who looked so seriously unwell that all thoughts of Jack and Imogen had got instantly filed under 'later' when she'd arrived fifteen minutes ago.

Her boyfriend, Paul, hovered anxiously, wiping his girlfriend's brow with a damp cloth.

'How long have you been feeling like this, Lara?'

She groaned and grabbed a bowl, vomiting into it.

Paul wrung his hands. 'She has sore tummy for a long time now.'

'How long?'

'Since we leave Indonesia. She feel sick some days, and then she is OK for a few days, and then sick again with diarrhoea.'

Travelling through Asia meant the chance of picking up something like Giardia or another parasitic infection was high, and Lara's symptoms right up until now matched that of the more chronic pattern of a parasite. She took Lara's pulse again: thready and tachycardic. This was an acute case of something. She turned back to Paul. 'Sick like this?'

'No, no. This only for two days. She vomits for two days and eats nothing. She tell me it is her—' Paul's ears pinked up '—her woman's monthly, but she has never been like this before.'

Sophie nodded, agreeing that severe dehydration and vomiting bile wasn't usually caused by dysmenorrhoea. She took the bowl from Lara's hands and helped her lie down again. 'I need to feel your tummy, OK?'

Lara seemed barely able to nod.

She palpated the woman's abdomen, her fingers hitting a bloated, rigid abdominal wall, and the woman flinched. 'Lara, have you used your bowels recently?'

'I think she is too sick to concentrate on English.' Paul translated into German and Lara's hands fluttered around her face in embarrassment as she replied. 'She says she has had diarrhoea very badly today.'

Sophie patted her patient's hand. There was nothing worse than being a million miles away from everything that was familiar and being desperately ill. She wrapped the blood-pressure cuff around Lara's arm and listened to the whoosh and thrub of the blood pounding against the arteries. She checked it a second time, hoping she'd missed the systolic reading the first time. She hadn't. It was far too low.

High fever, low blood-pressure and a bloated and rigid abdominal wall. As she placed her stethoscope onto Lara's abdomen, she heard a knock on the door.

Paul opened it and she heard Jack's melodic voice introducing himself.

Her heart skipped a beat and she immediately shut out the sound of his voice and concentrated on Lara's bowel sounds, or lack of bowel sounds; the normal gurgle she expected to hear was absent.

As she pulled the stethoscope out of her ears, she smelt Jack's clean, fresh scent of soap and sunshine before she heard his softly spoken words stroking her behind her ear.

'Sophie.'

The deep timbre of his voice sent a tingle racing through her, fleetingly touching every part of her before diving deep and settling in to vibrate her core. She swung the stethoscope around her neck, steadying herself before she glanced up into intense and serious mauve eyes that shimmered with traces of blue. Her stomach jolted.

She'd stared deeply into those eyes a few hours ago and lost herself in their sizzling thrill and passion, but now only the colour was familiar, the gaze being only professional and remote. It wasn't just the gaze that was different. Everything else about him had utterly changed—how he held himself, how he dressed. The bad boy was no longer. Gone was the close-fitting white T-shirt and the glorious black-leather trousers. In their place he wore a short-sleeved, blue-and-white, broad-striped shirt and navy-blue knee-length shorts, held against his hips by a plain leather belt with a simple silver buckle. His hair, which had struck her as unusually neat when he'd worn leathers, now perfectly suited the crisp and pressed image of a country doctor who took life seriously. Very seriously.

Like Simon: the sort of man she avoided at all costs.

She bit her lip again. It was like staring at a stranger, and deep down inside her something battled hard not to shed a tear of loss.

'Imogen's being cared for by the receptionist so I'm here to give you a hand.' His tone was all business, as if they were colleagues who'd just met.

She huffed out a breath. Technically, she supposed they *had* just met. She matched his businesslike tone. 'I need the defibrillator from the truck.'

'Right. Done.' Jack gave her a curt nod, one that said he understood the urgency, and stepped out of the room.

'What is wrong?'

Paul must have caught the worried glance she'd given

Jack. Sophie wasn't totally certain about her diagnosis, but what Lara needed right now was standard emergency treatment: airway; breathing; circulation. 'Lara's very dehydrated and needs fluids.'

She quickly found the tourniquet, a litre of Hartmann's electrolyte solution and an IV pack inside the emergency medical-kit, and primed the tubing. She handed the bag to Paul. 'Find something to hang that off, or stand there and hold it high.'

'I will be the pole.' Despite his palpable fear, he nobly raised his arm, holding it above his head so the fluid could flow as soon as the valve was opened.

It took her three attempts to find a vein, her fingers probing desperately for one that hadn't collapsed, and she'd only just slid the cannula into Lara's leg when Jack returned with the requested machine.

He gently placed the dots on the half-conscious woman's chest. 'She's dehydrated, so ectopic beats are expected with gastro.'

Sophie watched his long, deft fingers connecting the electrodes and tried valiantly to block out the image of those wondrous hands caressing her body to fever pitch, and how their touch had separated her body and mind in a spiral of bone melting bliss. This was the exact reason why a girl wasn't supposed to re-meet a casual lover. Sophie leaned in and said, *sotto voce*, 'I'm expecting arrhythmias.'

His brows shot to his hairline as he stared at the small screen of the defibrillator. 'What's your diagnosis? Obviously more than gastro.'

Sophie tugged on a curl. 'It's a confusing picture. She's got a fever, guarded abdomen, is vomiting bile and has no bowel sounds, but earlier today she had uncontrollable diarrhoea. Added into that mix, she's been travelling in Asia, but I'm now thinking that could be a red herring.'

Jack remained silent but his forehead creased into a deep frown as he ran the symptoms through his head. Sophie saw the moment he came to her conclusion. 'The diarrhoea aside, it sounds like a bowel obstruction and peritonitis.'

'Exactly, so I'll stabilise and evacuate. But Barragong is two hours by road.'

Jack shook his head. 'This young woman needs to go to Flinders Medical Centre asap.'

Sophie had no idea where that was, so she delegated according to knowledge. Jack knew exactly who to ring.

'Can you organise that while I insert a naso-gastric tube, put in a second line and start her on broad-spectrum antibiotics?'

He gave her a grim nod and turned to Paul. 'Lara's very ill, mate, and we're going to evacuate her by plane to Adelaide.'

Paul paled under his tan. 'I must go with her.'

'Of course. There's usually room on the plane for one relative.' Jack clapped his hand onto the young man's shoulders. 'Keep holding those IV bags up and I'll ring the flying doctors. Back soon.'

As Sophie pulled the trocar out of an IV cannula and connected up the second drip, she wished she had access to a lab so she knew exactly where Lara's blood chemistry was at, but given the runs of arrhythmias it was seriously out of whack. Balancing the correct amount of potassium without under-administering or over-administering was like tip-toeing through a minefield so she had to depend on the amount in the Hartmanns to do the job. 'Lara, I have to slide this tube into your nose and down your throat. Try and breathe long, deep breaths for me.'

Lara's eyes fluttered, and Sophie's breath stalled as her gaze swung to the ECG reading, but the expected run of arrhythmias was thankfully absent. Lara's barely rouse-able state was currently due to the high fever and the suspected mess of bowel contents in her peritoneum. Not that it made it any less of a concern; Lara was desperately ill and needed surgery sooner rather than later.

'We're in luck.' Jack burst into the room all energy and organisation. 'There's a crew just finished a clinic at Mootabrook Station so they're diverting to us.'

Half an hour later, Sophie watched her very first flying-doctor's plane with its distinctive blue-and-red stripes take off into a dusky, red-streaked, outback sky. She'd been both amazed and relieved at the set-up of the plane as an airborne intensive-care unit; hopefully they'd get Lara to Adelaide before she deteriorated any more. 'How long does it ta—?' She turned towards Jack but her question died on her lips. He was no longer standing next her. In fact, he was fast disappearing back towards the hotel, plumes of red dust rising from his heels. What on earth?

She rubbed her temples, the long, long day catching up with her; it was hard to believe she'd only got off the bus nine hours ago. Thankfully her job here was done. She'd delivered the little girl to Jack, and Imogen was now his responsibility. Sophie could return to Barragong. Alone.

Blessedly alone.

She absently scratched her arm, recalling the trip with Imogen who'd constantly asked her questions and had wanted her to hold conversations with the toy emu that looked like it needed a jolly good wash. *Just shut up, Sophie, you're not Mum.*

She shut out her younger sister's voice. Sophie knew that she and kids didn't match, and the journey with Imogen had stressed her more than dealing with casualties of war, so she was glad she didn't have to do a repeat performance. The thought of returning to the lovely homestead and having it all to herself wrapped around her like a warm blanket on a cold night.

As for leaving Jack behind, well he'd made that unexpectedly easy. Not one trace of the man she'd been so inextricably drawn to existed any more. She ached for the loss of all that wicked charm.

A jet of anger spouted up, fizzing in her veins. OK, so it was pretty uncomfortable meeting up again so soon after completely uninhibited sex, especially as they'd never planned to meet again—but it wasn't like she'd come chasing after him. She'd been forced to find him because of the child, and she had no intention of hanging around and intruding on his holiday. Her being here certainly didn't warrant rude avoidance tactics like this or a complete personality change.

It was like a stranger had moved right in.

And right now that stranger was royally ticking her off with the way he was storming towards the residence section of the hotel as if she didn't exist. Well, she had a few questions she needed to ask him before she left, and not just about Lara. With a quick jog, she caught him up. 'How long will it take for the plane to get to Adelaide?'

He didn't slow his gait. 'With this weather, about an hour, and the bowel surgeon's ready and waiting for her, so she'll go straight to Theatre.'

'That long?' Man, Australia was a big country. 'Will the surgeon ring?'

Jack snorted—an unexpectedly sharp and bitter sound. 'No. We're the country doctors, so it's our job to ring him.'

The harsh, half-laugh settled over Sophie like a prickle, making her frown. 'That sounds almost disillusioned.'

He dodged her seeking eyes and ran a hand through his hair, his jaw clenched tight-white. '*That's* why I need a holiday.'

Perfect segue. 'Right. About that holiday—you seem to have forgotten someone.'

He stopped abruptly, the blue of his eyes sparking a deep and dramatic violet like the rays of the setting sun. 'Of course I didn't forget someone.'

'Then why was a child literally dumped at the house? The mother didn't even come inside.' Righteous anger bubbled inside her. 'If I hadn't been there, Imogen would have been totally alone. Why would the woman act like that?'

'Because her mother is am immature, self-centred—' He pulled in a breath, visibly stopping himself from saying anything more.

Protecting her? Why? Past lover? Ex-wife? 'Is Imogen your daughter?'

'No!' The word, loaded with indignation and effrontery, shot out of his mouth like the bullet from a gun. 'God, you think I'd leave town without considering the care of my child?'

She tried not to sway backwards as the force of his words hit her in the chest. 'I have no idea what to think. We hardly know each other.'

A flash of the man she'd tumbled into bed with

surfaced for a fraction of a second and a sizzle of her own heat scorched her. But almost instantly his cool, professional persona shot back into place, dousing her reaction like water against flames, and leaving her unsettled and fidgety. She tilted her chin. 'Let me rephrase that: just because we had sex, it doesn't mean I know what your values and ethics are.'

He stiffened; it was like every word he spoke was being chiselled out of him. 'My mother, who also lives at Armitage House, is a registered foster carer and Imogen comes to us for respite care. I'm registered as well, as I live in the house, but Mum—Min—is really the main care-giver. She notified the authorities that she wasn't available for three weeks in December and she told Kylie, Imogen's mother. I have no idea why Kylie left Imogen with you, but thank you for bringing her here; I'll deal with it.'

'Brilliant. I'm glad it's all sorted.' Her words rushed out, clipped and brisk with relief. Thankfully she was now off the hook as far as Imogen was concerned. But the unsettled, edgy feeling that should have disappeared now she knew the whole story didn't fade. It not only stayed with her, it grew stronger.

Quicksand warning. Soft cliff-edge. Avalanche area. Time to leave. Get out now.

She was an expert at leaving and she recognised the signs to go. 'Well, it's a long drive back, so I'll say goodbye.' Her hand shot out automatically for a handshake before she realised how ludicrous that was given what had gone down between them.

He stared at her hand hovering between them, watching it drop back by her side. 'There's no need for goodbyes, Sophie.'

Her head shot up, her gaze meeting those piercing

eyes, and despite their complete absence of wild fun her heart somehow hammered ridiculously hard against her ribs. 'Excuse me?'

Resignation crossed his face and he sighed. 'I need you to drive me and Imogen back to Barragong.'

No, no, no, no, no. Sex and goodbye—that was the deal. The goddess of free love had the decency to look sheepish and apologetic.

Words poured out on a stream of agitation. 'But you're on holidays; you have the motorcycle and your mobile phone so surely you can sort the problem out from here?'

'The problem?' His eyes flashed with judgement as a vein throbbed in his neck. 'Imogen is a *child*, not a problem.'

She tugged at a curl and slammed it hard behind her ear as the feeling of being chastened by her school mistress took her back fifteen years in a heartbeat. 'I didn't mean to infer—'

He raised his hand to silence her. 'Whatever. The case worker wants Imogen back in Barragong tomorrow and that means me too. The problem is that it's sensibly illegal for a child under the age of eight to ride pillion on a motorcycle. As I thought I was on holidays and not going anywhere tonight, I've had a few beers, so driving is out of the question and that's why we need you to drive us back.'

His words rained down on her, full of precise organisation, and she struggled to connect all the dots. 'Right… tomorrow.' The day that came after this night. The day she'd expected to wake up all alone in Armitage House to start her stint in Barragong. But now she'd awaken to face a man she'd thrown herself at because she'd never expected to see him again. A man who was looking at her now as if she was completely asexual and just part of his current problem. She stifled a groan, hoping the red earth beneath her feet would open and up and swallow her.

It was like he'd read her mind and, without a glimmer of the lust that had shone so brightly in his eyes earlier in the day, he stared at her, his stance practical and no-nonsense. 'I don't like this any more than you do. Hell, this is supposed to be *my* holiday, and if I could avoid going back I would. It's one night. You take the back wing of the house and Imogen and I will be in the front. I promise we won't even see each other in the morning before you leave for work.

'By the time you get home, Imogen will be in the care of a foster family and I'll be gone.' His attempt at a smile didn't quite come off. 'It's just a slight hiccup in our original plan of goodbye, and we're adults, right? We can do this?'

'Sure.' But her heart tugged strangely at the empty look in his eyes and she wished she could put back the spark that had greeted her so enthusiastically a short nine hours ago.

CHAPTER FIVE

JACK had developed a loathing for his phone. 'Yes, I'll hold.' He ground out the words, trying to maintain his veneer of civility. He'd spent most of the day either caring for Imogen, or in the home office on the phone. He'd been dealing with bureaucrats, social workers, case managers and the police, trying to find out where Kylie had vanished to and trying to find a foster family who could care for Imogen. Trying to sort things out so he could leave town.

He had squat.

As promised, he'd stayed out of Sophie's way since they'd arrived back last night. He'd only caught a couple of glimpses of her, which was the only thing going his way right now. Every time he saw her he was reminded of the tickle of her hair, the way her exotic scent scudded rampant desire through his veins, and how wonderful it had felt making love to her.

Don't go there. It's never going to happen again.

He was leaving in the morning. He had to. He should have been gone already, but everything had taken longer than he'd wanted it to. He tugged at the collar on his polo shirt and silently breathed, 'Hurry up,' into the phone. It was four-forty-five in the afternoon and he was close to a solution; he was sure of it.

'Dr Armitage.' The too-calm voice of Carmel, the social worker, grated against his frustration. 'Sorry for the delay, but there are no new developments. We'll continue to try and locate Kylie, but even if we find her we have grave concerns about returning Imogen to her care. Given Kylie's recent behaviour, coupled with last year's episode, we feel that it wouldn't be in Imogen's best interest for her to return to her mother. We've drawn up the paperwork making arrangements for on-going foster care until Kylie makes a choice. Either she accepts our help and works towards being deemed a fit parent, or she decides she no longer wants to raise her child. Given her history there's a strong chance she may wish to place Imogen into permanent care.'

He ploughed his hand through his hair. 'You're not telling me anything I don't already know. I agree, Imogen needs stability, and a foster family would give her that.'

Carmel made a sympathetic murmuring sound before pausing for a beat. Goose bumps instantly rose on Jack's arm.

'Jack, we could place Imogen with another family, but that would mean her leaving Barragong and I'm sure you'll agree that really isn't in the best interests of the child. We're certain that isn't what either you or your mother would want. We really appreciate you caring for Imogen while your mother's on her well-earned holiday and I'm sure it's what she'd want as well.'

What about my well-earned holiday? But voices from the past suddenly started talking over him, competing for air space in his head. His father's warmth: *Jack, as doctors we don't just treat the sick in this town. We're a moral compass, a barometer of social conscience—it's our duty.*

Mary's ultimatum: *Jack, it's me or this town.*

His own voice: *It's my life too.*

'Jack?' Imogen, clutching Sheils and a large piece of paper, peeked around the door before running over to him and climbing onto his lap.

The voices muted into an uneasy silence as all the tightly wound frustration seeped out of him and a sudden, unsteady peace took its place. He blew out a long, decision-making breath, said goodbye and ended the call. He couldn't fight it any longer. Imogen's welfare was first and foremost and he grudgingly accepted he was in Barragong until his mother returned. The town had won this round, but he wasn't giving up on his long-awaited holiday. He'd get the bike delivered from Parachilna and he'd take off again on New Year's Day. He smiled at the thought. A new year and a new start—it held a certain cosmic rightness.

He ruffled Imogen's hair. 'Did you finish your picture? Let's take a look.'

She rolled it out on the desk. A bright-yellow sun, a wobbly house and a red stick-figure.

'Who's that?'

'Santa.' She stared up at him, her brown eyes strikingly similar to Sophie's. 'Jack, will Santa find me here?'

His heart ripped for this little girl whose unstable life meant she had no idea where she was living week to week. He mightn't be able to take his longed-for trip but he loved Christmas and it would be no problem at all to give Imogen the best Christmas season a kid could have. 'Let's write Santa a letter right now and tell him that you're going to be at Min and Jack's house.'

She clapped her hands and snuggled in closer as if her whole body had just relaxed. 'And Sophie's.'

Sophie.

His fledgling peace shattered like glass and he swallowed a groan against a constricted throat. How could he have forgotten Sophie? The dynamically gorgeous, free-spirited Sophie, who with one look from those chocolate eyes had him hard and wanting. Sharing a house with her would be like the temptation of a Christmas gift under the tree, all wrapped and waiting, and him not being allowed to open it. This situation was the *very* reason he avoided liaisons in Barragong. In town, he was the doctor. Outside of town he was Jack, and no one in Barragong knew what he got up to and that way no one talked about it. Mary's departure had given them a field day and he was never giving the town that sort of gossip power again.

Avoiding Sophie for less than a day had been possible. Avoiding her for a month while sharing a house with her would be totally impossible. He dropped his head onto Imogen's dark curls. How had his holiday just turned into an endurance test?

A prickly sensation brushed Sophie's bare arm and she jumped, her fingers batting at the feeling.

Diana laughed. 'It's not a spider, it's just tinsel. The pin holding it on the ceiling must have fallen down.'

Leave the tinsel up, Sophie, so Christopher can enjoy it when he comes home. The ghost of her mother's voice made Sophie shiver and she didn't try to explain that a spider would have been preferable to the Christmas decoration. She'd been totally unprepared for the hospital's Christmas-decoration onslaught that had taken place overnight. 'I'm surprised you decorate.'

The pregnant nurse stared at her as if she'd just landed from another planet. 'It's December.'

Sophie tried to laugh off her anxieties. 'I know, but it's summer here, so hardly Christmassy.'

Diana spoke patiently as if she was explaining to a child. 'We mightn't have cold weather, open fires and snow, but it's still Christmas.' She gave an encouraging smile. 'It's a great time for you to be here, and just you wait, we'll get you involved in everything so you'll have a totally memorable Aussie Christmas.'

Sophie's chest tightened and the need to leave pummelled her. *You left Asia for this?* She breathed in slowly. How dumb had she been, thinking that because December fell in summer in Australia it would mean Christmas wasn't a big deal? She abruptly closed the file on the computer and jumped to her feet, needing to get out of the walls that seemed to be closing in on her. 'I have to go, but ring me if Mrs Retallick's temperature goes up.'

Without waiting for Diana's reply, she walked quickly out into the heat, gulped in air and headed for the four-wheel-drive. She turned up the air conditioner full blast, turned up the music full blast, threw the gearstick into drive and pulled onto the road, heading to Armitage House.

Jack will be gone, Jack will be gone.

She realised with a start that she'd put those four words into a chant in time with the beat of the music. If willing him to be gone worked, then he'd be long gone by now, and he *had* to be gone. She needed the house to herself; after the hospital's decoration frenzy she desperately needed a tinsel-free zone.

She hadn't heard from Jack but she hadn't expected to because the situation with the child had nothing to do with her. He wanted so badly to be gone from Barragong that she had every faith he'd have sorted things out and taken off again on his long-awaited trip.

She relaxed into the drive and almost missed the turn-off. With a spray of gravel, she pulled hard left at the yellow-barrel post box and caught a flash of red and green, but she was going too fast to really see what it was. She glimpsed more flashes of red and green in the trees and slowed down, fascinated by the colourful birds with green backs and red, blue and yellow stripes on their chests. She'd have to look them up in one of the bird books in the homestead's library. As she crossed the cattle grid, she held her breath, and then in a delicious rush of relief she let it go. The circular drive was empty. No car. No motorcycle.

Thank you.

She opened the front door and the coolness trapped by the thick stone walls welcomed her home. She dropped her bag and keys on the massive hall stand, and delight rushed through her. She'd have a lemon, lime and bitters out by the pool, enjoy a swim and then barbeque herself a steak. Life was good. Like an excited child, she started to dance down the very long hall.

'Put the angel on top.' Imogen's high, sweet voice drifted down the hall.

'The angel it is, sweetheart.' Laughter clung to Jack's baritone rumble.

Sophie stopped so fast she almost teetered over her toes and her blood swooped to her feet. She swayed and grabbed at the doorway's architrave.

'Sophie.' Imogen ran over to her and grabbed her hand. 'Look at what Jack and me did. There's lights too.' With her large brown eyes shining, the child tugged her towards the biggest *faux* fir Christmas tree Sophie had ever seen in a house.

Her mouth dried as she took in the tree dripping with baubles and tinsel, and then it parched completely when her gaze focussed on Jack. He stood on the top of a ladder with a star in one hand and an angel in the other. Sunlight poured through the bay window, picking up the traces of silver tinsel and cobwebs that clung to his polo shirt and the streak of dirt that dusted his cheek. Gone was the *über*-uptight doctor who had appeared last night in Parachilna. Right now he looked like her rumpled, dark-haired god whose brooding good looks would instantly tarnish all the gold of the angels with a glance from those stunning eyes.

Her lungs cramped.

Imogen tugged at her hand. 'Isn't it beautiful?'

Yes, he is.

'You can touch it if you're careful,' Imogen instructed.

Leave the tree, alone, Sophie. Nobody touches the tree.

'No.' The word shot out of her mouth harsh and loud, and Imogen's face fell. Sophie bit her lip and tried to steady her ragged breathing.

Jack put the angel on the very top of the tree and with calf-muscles flexing came quickly down the ladder. Without looking at Sophie, he bobbed down so he was at eye level with Imogen, his dimple twinkling in his cheek. 'I think Sophie's a bit surprised that we've done such a great job so quickly, but we'll finish this tomorrow. How about you watch a Christmas DVD while I talk to Sophie?'

Imogen stared longingly at the box with a picture of a train on it and hesitated, her bottom lip drooping slightly. She finally looked back at Jack, her expression half-resigned. 'OK.'

She picked up her emu and Jack walked her to the TV room. He returned a moment later, closing the hall door firmly behind him, the aloof stranger firmly back in place. It was like he was two different people in one gorgeous package.

Sophie finally found her voice, although her brain was still playing catch-up. 'You're still here.'

He shrugged. 'I am.' He rounded the island bench and pulled open the fridge door. 'I think you need a drink.'

She folded her arms across her chest, mostly to stop herself from shaking. 'I'm on call.'

He grimaced. 'You're on call for this damn town for the next three months, but tonight we both need a drink.' He twisted the black cap off a green wine-bottle and poured two glasses of sauvignon blanc. The only sounds in the room were the glug of the wine, the ticking of the clock and the hum of the fridge.

'Take a seat.' Cool and polite, he carried the bottle and glasses on a tray and motioned her to the couch.

She didn't move. She didn't want to sit. His overly restrained energy, the tone of voice, his instructions—everything about him reminded her of Simon. This starchy Jack completely unnerved her. She'd been much more relaxed around the bad boy, who by default had expected nothing of her and from whom in turn she'd expected nothing. She stared, hoping to glimpse the man she'd seen for a moment at the top of the ladder, because then she'd find the man she'd slept with.

'Sit, Sophie.'

The command was unmistakeable and much to her chagrin she sat down hard—not because she wanted to but because her knees had buckled under her as the trickles of dread in her veins morphed into a cascade.

Her fingers closed around the proffered stem of the wine glass, deliberately avoiding Jack's. He sat down at the far end of the three-seater couch, but it wasn't far enough away, and his masculine scent and aura slammed into her as if the distance between them was mere millimetres rather than sixty centimetres.

She forced herself to speak. 'You're not leaving, are you?'

'No.'

She drained her half-filled glass in one long gulp and with a shaking hand put it down on the coffee table.

Jack cleared his throat. 'Imogen needs some sort of security, and until my mother gets back from her cruise and we plan for the future I'm it.'

You got through last night, what's another day or so?

Last night we didn't have a Christmas wonderland.

'When exactly does she get back?'

'Christmas Eve.'

'Christmas Eve.' She heard the screech in her voice, as loud and as harsh as a galah. 'That's three weeks away.' Her heart hammered and her vision swam as control raced away from her. Now she had the trifecta: a Christmas tree, a child, and a man she'd technically had sex with, except that wild and glorious man had vanished and a serious man had appeared in his place. Her eczema prickled.

Leave, leave.

Breathe. Breathe.

Jack reached for a folder on the coffee table. 'Believe me, I know *exactly* how far away it is, and with that in mind, and so we can share the house in a mature way, I've drawn up a roster.'

A roster? She thought of the procedure folder and the 'useful OCD folder' and realised with devastating clarity that his receptionist hadn't made them up. Jack had: the remote and organising Jack who'd appeared yesterday when she'd delivered Imogen to him. Reality dumped on her like an icy bath. This man was no stranger—this was who Jack really was. How had she missed the signs?

You only wanted to see the bad boy.

She gave a strangled laugh. 'You've got a roster. Of course you have.'

His brow wrinkled. 'Pardon?'

She poured herself a full glass of wine and took another long sip, feeling the warmth of the alcohol trickle through her. If she'd wanted to have her life organised and ordered, she could have stayed with Simon. Hell, she'd only slept with Jack because he'd had a wild energy about him and a devil-may-care attitude, and because she knew he'd walk away and would never want her to stay. This sanitised version of Jack reminded her too much of Simon, too much of heartache, and it made her edgy. He had no right to change on her like this. If she was to survive sharing a Christmas-themed house with him and a child then, damn it, she wanted the old Jack back. Running wild with *that* Jack was the only thing that would keep her from going completely crazy.

'The Jack I met yesterday didn't give a damn about folders and rosters. In fact, if he was here he'd be tearing my clothes off right now.'

For a brief moment his irises darkened to navy and flashed with undisguised lust.

You found him. He wasn't hiding very far away at all. The goddess gave her a high five, but before the clap was over his eyes cooled and then blanked like a screen dropping into place.

He jerkily refilled his glass. 'That Jack was on holidays, expecting to leave town for three months, and he wasn't responsible for a child.' The muscles on his neck tightened as he seemed to grab a deep breath. 'Please don't take this personally, Sophie, but as the town's doctors nothing else can happen between us.'

She blinked twice, not certain she'd heard him correctly. 'Doctors can't have sex? I think we disproved that theory yesterday.'

He shifted in his seat, clearly uncomfortable. 'Not in Barragong we can't. This is a small town, Sophie. People look up to us to set an example.'

Laughter bubbled up at the old-fashioned attitude coming from a guy in his early thirties, and then died on her lips as she read the serious set of his shoulders. 'Oh my God, you really believe that. That's crazy, Jack. Who gets married to have sex any more? This is now, and no one cares who's having sex with whom, or if they're getting it in or out of marriage, or both.'

'In Barragong they do.' He drained his glass. 'This is a small town and marriage is the expected commitment. It's fine for you—you'll stay for three months and then leave, but I live here. My family's been part of this community for a very long time and I protect its integrity. All my liaisons take place out of town.'

She couldn't believe what she was hearing but then she thought about the guest book she'd read, filled with the signatures of dignitaries and luminaries. She remembered how fast he'd changed yesterday when he knew he was coming back to Barragong. He'd completely buried every aspect of his personality that had drawn her to him and she wondered about the constraints that bound him. 'You don't have sex in Barragong? No wonder you tore my clothes off yesterday.'

'Sophie.'

Her name came out as a half-growl of warning and a half-moan of need, instantly sending delicious shivers shooting along her spine. The wild part of Jack was still there and he still wanted her. She clutched at that thought hard and fast, and smiled, because it was the *only* thing in this whole situation that was keeping her from bolting out of the door, and it was the only thing worth smiling about.

Why did the woman have to smile at him like that? Sitting on this couch, breathing in her perfume, watching the way her hair constantly brushed her smooth, white cheeks was killing him, and Jack had three weeks of this ahead of him. The memory of her wrapped around him sang in his veins and as he tried hard to shut down the sensation his words came out pompous and self-righteous. 'It's not just the town. We have a child in the house to consider.'

Her wide mouth flattened out and she rubbed her temples as a sigh shuddered out of her. 'This is a mess, Jack.'

There it was again, that high-class accent unexpectedly calling a spade a spade. Whether it be sex or work she was remarkably frank and he appreciated her open take on the whole uncomfortable situation. For the first time since she'd walked into the room he relaxed, sensing her acceptance that they could get through the next few weeks as he planned—platonic housemates and colleagues.

He leaned back on the couch. 'You're not wrong there, Soph.' He flipped open the folder. 'But we can make it work.'

Her gaze seemed fixed on the folder but then she raised it to his, her expression unexpectedly guarded.

'Seeing as you're setting ground-rules, I have some of my own.'

The brisk, British nanny that surfaced occasionally and was so at odds with her usual free-sprit style was back. As she sat up a bit straighter he noticed her looking at the Christmas tree and rubbing her inner elbow. He'd seen her do that when she'd treated Lochie and then again on the drive back to Barragong with Imogen.

He clicked his pen open and grinned. 'Let me guess. You want in on the Christmas decorating. Don't worry, the tree is just the tip of the iceberg, there are six more boxes in the roof space. If there's one thing the Armitages do well, it's Christmas.'

Her head swung towards him so fast it could have caused whiplash, and her lush brown irises lost out to a sea of black. 'I try to ignore Christmas, so I'll leave the decorating to you and Imogen.'

'Ignore Christmas?' He laughed at the absurdity. 'Sorry, but this year that's going to be impossible. As the town's doctor you have to open Carols by Candlelight and ride on the County Fire Service's fire truck with Santa.'

Her lithe body stiffened. 'If you love Christmas so much I wouldn't dream of taking that honour away from you, so consider it yours.' She tilted her chin upwards in a jerky movement, and a moment later her breasts rose, straining against her Indian top as she took in a deep breath.

A vision of white, silky skin, the feel of full and heavy breasts against his palms and rosebud nipples in his mouth thundered through him, stealing all the blood from his brain.

'…with Imogen.'

He saw Sophie's lips move but the roar of desire

charging through his body had drowned out her words. He fought hard to concentrate, trying to pull together what she'd said about Christmas and Imogen. 'I beg your pardon?'

She swallowed hard. 'I want to make it very clear that, just because I'm a woman and we're sharing a house, please don't think that I'm automatically going to be doing housework, and taking care of Imogen for you. I'm Barragong's doctor and that's my priority.'

Surprise rocked him, sending lust scurrying, and irritation slid in taking its place. 'I'm not a chauvinistic bastard who expects women to do everything, Sophie. I figured we'd share the housework.' He shot her a smile. 'And the odd bit of help with Imogen would be appreciated.'

She didn't return his smile. 'Jack, I signed up to be Barragong's doctor and that's all. Not withstanding emergencies, Imogen's your job.' Rising to her feet, her hair swung around her, masking her face. For the first time since he'd met her she didn't brush it away.

'Jack, I'm hungry.' Imogen ran into the room, cutting off his question to Sophie about why she was so adamant about this.

'So am I.' He scooped her up into his arms and pretended to gnaw on her arm. 'Num, num, num, you're tasty.'

Imogen squealed with delight and then shot him an indignant look. 'You can't eat me, Jack. I'm a girl.'

He gently tweaked her nose. 'So you are. Well, I guess we need some dinner. Sophie, I'm cooking, so what do you fancy for dinner?' He swung around, expecting to find her where she'd been standing a moment ago, but the room was empty.

He sat Imogen down on the island bench. 'Looks

like it's just us, Im.' But as he stared into the fridge his thoughts were fixed on Sophie's stand on Christmas and occasional babysitting. What the hell was up with that?

CHAPTER SIX

AS DAWN'S long fingers of sunshine reached across the desert, the light cued the flock of galahs in the large gum-tree in the home paddock, sending them screeching across a rosy sky. Sophie groaned and pulled her pillow around her ears. Didn't they know it was Sunday, the only day of the week she didn't have to be at the clinic at eight a.m.? She rolled over, realising she no longer woke in fright at the noise. Barragong's peace was slowly filtering through her veins.

But she couldn't fall back to sleep so she swung her legs over the edge of the bed and pulled on her running togs. With a quick lace of her shoes, she took off on a five-kilometre run in the cool of the early morning. One week in Barragong and she was easily under the spell of the outback. She loved being out in the red desert with the crimson-and-mauve sunrise and only kangaroos and emus for company, although if she was brutally honest the emus gave her the creeps.

Her daily run kept her sane. She ran out her frustrations that she was sharing a house with a man she hardly recognised—yet the bad boy in Jack surfaced now and then in looks and glances, making her ache for him and making her wish it happened more often. She ran to keep the Christmas demons at bay now she was living in a house where every surface had a Christmas ornament on it. All in all, the running had been working well, along with limited contact with both Jack and Imogen. They shared some meals when she wasn't working long hours at the clinic and the hospital. Using the excuse of exhaustion, she deliberately wore herself out so she could lose herself in the oblivion of sleep. Not that she'd slept that well. Every time she closed her eyes Jack came to her in her dreams, but the dreams didn't come close to matching the reality of the man who'd taken her to dizzying heights. She woke feeling fidgety and on edge, which was why she ran.

As she reached the outer buildings on her return, she saw a flash of silver coming from the garage and she jogged over to check it out. Shirtless but wearing a pair of old jersey-shorts, Jack was arranging a silvery-grey cover over his recently returned motorcycle. Golden muscles rippled as he tucked and pulled and she slowed to a walk, silently soaking in the sight.

He turned at the sound of her feet against the gravel and immediately his eyes ate her up with a long sweeping gaze that touched all of her but lingered on the low-cut style of her running singlet. Instantly, all the hard work of her run vanished as every particle of sexual frustration returned in a tingling flood. His crazy, self-imposed 'no sex' rule was driving them both insane, and putting them both on edge.

She tossed her head and met his look, giving him a wide smile, ever hopeful the wild Jack would return and she could lose herself in great sex—that would really help her get through the horror that was December and keep the haunting memories at bay.

'You're up early.'

His prosaic words stole the wondrous, wild gleam

from his eyes and she almost sobbed. She wanted him back to play with, so she played dirty, wanting to tempt him, knowing the memory of what had happened between them the one time she'd ridden that bike would be high in his mind. 'Putting the bike to bed? That's a shame.'

Desire flashed bright again in his eyes but a muscle twitched in his jaw. 'It's the sensible thing to do, seeing as I can't ride it.'

She frowned as she thought about the week just past. Jack had run the house and cared for Imogen with unending patience, something she knew totally eluded her. He was organised, neat and methodical. And caged. So much tension vibrated from him she could almost hear him buzzing, and she knew he wasn't happy. Neither of them was happy. For some reason he truly believed he had to be Barragong's model citizen and she wanted to know why. 'You're big on sensible, aren't you, Jack?' *Except when you thought you were leaving town and you scorched the sheets with me.*

He gave the cover a sharp tug. 'I have responsibilities.'

'Oh, please, we all have those. It doesn't mean you can't have fun.' She walked over and ran her hand along the seat, remembering how wonderful it had been having the desert wind in her face and the heat on her skin. 'You can still ride her, Jack, you're just choosing not too.'

He folded his arms across his chest and this time his eyes flashed with anger. 'I have a child to take care of, remember? I do believe your words were, "Imogen's your job".'

She didn't take the bait because that would lead to questions about her family and it was much easier not to talk about them. 'Imogen goes to kindergarten four half-days a week and that gives you a few hours in the day to relax and be yourself. So for heaven's sake, loosen up, take a ride and start enjoying your holiday.'

His inky brows drew down like a stormy cloud. 'My holiday? That's rich. A holiday means leaving this bloody town, Soph, and yet I'm still here. Again!' He grabbed his T-shirt and stomped back toward the house, pulling the wire door open with unnecessary force.

His fury socked her in the chest and a wave of sympathy rolled through her. He seemed to have a love-hate relationship with the town. How naïve she'd been to think the Jack she'd met on that first day was an uncomplicated, fun-loving thrill seeker. He had more facets to him than a diamond and each one of them fascinated her. She jogged towards the house and found him thumping around the kitchen making coffee. Only Jack could wear a faded and shapeless T-shirt and make it look like a fashion statement. 'What do you mean you're still here *again*?'

He peeled the top off the ground coffee and spooned it into the plunger, the pungent aroma filling the air. 'This isn't the first time I've planned this trip.' He leaned sideways, grabbed a folder off the crockery hutch and tossed it through the air at her like a Frisbee.

She caught it and saw a map on the cover outlining a route up through the centre of Australia and then into the many islands of Indonesia. It would be a totally brilliant journey on a motorcycle, an epic adventure, and one she wouldn't mind doing herself. As she read the point of origin, surprise made her look up. 'This trip was to start from Melbourne.'

He gave a wry smile. 'Yeah. That's where I was living and working five years ago. I actually got out of Barragong once.' The tang of bitterness clung to his words.

'So what stopped you taking the trip back then?'

The kettle screamed and Jack pulled it off the gas, pouring boiling water into the glass coffee-pot. He set the plunger into place, his face taut. 'My father's sudden and unexpected death from a ruptured aneurysm.'

Sophie's heart rolled over. 'Oh, Jack, I'm so sorry.'

He shook his head as if to say, 'I don't want sympathy' and he passed her a chopping board, a knife and a punnet of strawberries. 'Dad had been the GP here for years, and his father before him. Great-great grandfather and great-grandfather, who built this place, made a pile of money out of wool but the bottom dropped out of sheep, and a never-ending drought forced a career change.'

'The Armitages became doctors?' She hulled and sliced the berries as she listened.

'Got it in one.' Jack dropped four pieces of wholemeal bread into the large toaster.

She thought about family tradition and the implicit expectations that came with that. 'Did you want to become a doctor?'

'Absolutely.' He gave her a smile she'd never seen before. Devoid of the flirting and guile of the smiles that had greeted her arrival in town, and without any hint of the responsibility and seriousness she'd been seeing for the last week, this smile washed over her with genuine warmth. It immediately curled up inside her next to her heart, as if it belonged there.

Danger ahead.

Her knife slipped, slicing deeply into the flesh of her palm. She gasped as the acid from the berries stung like crazy, and she dropped the knife before racing to the sink. Trying to stem the flow of blood, she pressed her thumb against her palm, but a crimson river continued to trickle down her hand.

'That looks nasty.' Jack grabbed a first-aid kit out of a top cupboard and produced a wad of gauze. Pulling up two chairs, he sat her down and then firmly pressed the gauze into her palm before seating himself opposite her. He gave her a wink. 'Typical redhead.'

His touch was reassuring and unsettling in equal parts. 'Clumsy, or the fact I bleed like a stuck pig? You're right; I take ages to stop bleeding. Here, I'll do that.' She moved her hand, trying to hold the gauze.

He shook his head and kept his fingers firmly pressed against her palm, his tanned skin deliciously dark against her white. 'I'm the doctor, so do as you're told and let me look after you.'

His warmth rolled through her, making her giddy, and she fought against the desire to let her head fall forward onto his shoulder and shelter there. *You don't need a man in your life looking after you. They want too much in return.* She dragged in a breath, trying to find her control, trying to shed this terrifying feeling of closeness and instead find again the lust which usually protected her. Sex was uncomplicated; it was relationships that she ran from. She breathed in deep and fast. If she had to sit here with him so close, with their knees and foreheads almost touching, she needed a distraction. 'So if Armitage men become Barragong's doctors, why were you in Melbourne?'

'I went to boarding school in Melbourne for my senior years and then onto to Melbourne uni, and I stayed on for my residency, which then turned into being an A&E registrar. I loved the work. Dad and I had always talked in vague terms about me taking over the practice but it was a very long way down the track. I was living in

Carlton and loving it. Dad understood.' He grinned. 'Dad loved a party and he stayed away from Barragong for fifteen years.'

She thought about the streak of wildness she'd encountered when she'd first met Jack and how that had vanished so quickly when he knew he was staying in town. 'So your dad sowed all his wild oats before he came back here?'

Jack's head tilted slightly as if he'd never really thought about the question. 'I guess he did, because when he did come back to Barragong he came as a newlywed. Mind you, he was still living hard and fast when he met Mum. He and his mates had somehow managed to sneak into the nurses' home at Melbourne Central and Mum, being a good country girl, was used to looking after herself. She hit him hard with a rubber mallet and then had to do a head-injury chart on him for the next four hours.' He laughed, the sound deep and rich. 'They got married three months later.'

He bent his head to examine her palm by lifting the gauze, but blood immediately gushed. 'A bit longer still.'

Sophie smiled wistfully, loving the way his face had relaxed when he talked about his family. 'I like the sound of your mother.'

He nodded. 'Mum's pretty special, but then she had to be to survive living out here and sharing Dad with the *town*.'

Sophie frowned at the way he emphasised the word 'town' as if it was an unwelcome part of his life. 'Your mother's a foster carer, so it sounds like she shares herself with the town too.'

The pressure on her hand increased as tension rippled across his shoulders. 'She grew up in the country, so she knew what she was in for when she married into this family.' His face tightened. 'Not *everyone* gets it.'

A shiver ran through her. 'Who didn't get it, Jack?'

He stared at her for a moment as if weighing up options. 'My wife.'

A wife? She stared, then blinked. Twice. She hadn't seen that coming. *Think about it. It fits in perfectly with the model-citizen Jack.* 'You were married when your father died?'

He shook his head. 'No. I wasn't even engaged. Mary and I had been dating for a while and she'd been angling for a ring, but I had a trip to take. Marriage was the last thing on my mind, although I did invite her to come with me but she wasn't keen. She was a city girl, an advertising exec who didn't like dirt or dust and couldn't imagine life without her hair dryer. She didn't want me to go away, but she didn't want to come with me, so we were at an impasse.'

His dad had come back as a newlywed. Had he thought he needed to as well? 'But you proposed when you knew you were coming back to live and work in Barragong?'

He narrowed his eyes as if she'd just peeked inside a secret compartment and when he spoke his voice was tight. 'I realise with your roving lifestyle marriage might not be something you aspire to, but I didn't force Mary to marry me; it was what she wanted.' He snorted, the sound derisive and cynical. 'But her dream was short-lived as the reality of being my wife and sharing me with this town proved not to match her unrealistic dreams of the privileged life of landed gentry. This town doesn't make things easy, and the relationship rolled on to an acrimonious end two years later with her issuing me with an ultimatum that I choose her or the town.'

His raw hurt circled her and she bit her lip, thinking about Simon. 'Relationships are a minefield, and we all make mistakes, Jack.'

His gaze shot to hers, fast and penetrating. 'Who was yours?'

Her breath caught in her throat. How had being sympathetic ended up with the spotlight shining on her? She intended to swing it right back. 'His name was Simon, and he and I wanted different things out of life. Let's just say I totally get why this trip means so much to you. Sometimes you just have to get away, you know?'

'Oh yeah, I know.'

A thread of understanding spun out between them, tugging at her. She tried to resist it.

'I envy you your freedom, Soph—being able to go where the next job takes you. So how long since you were last in the UK?'

You're completely heartless, Sophie. She shut out Simon's voice. 'Two years.'

He glanced up, his eyes questioning. 'That's a long time. I would have thought seeing as your last job just finished you would have gone home to your family for Christmas.'

'I told you, I don't celebrate Christmas.' The words rushed out overly hasty.

Jack didn't blink. 'Hanukah, then?'

She shook her head, not wanting to answer his question. 'Surely I've stopped bleeding now.'

He gave her a long look and her heart hammered so hard against her ribs she felt certain he'd hear it. Finally he dropped his gaze back to her palm.

He eased the gauze back. 'Not good, Soph; I see the distinctive white of tendon. You're going to need stitches.'

'It can't possibly be that deep!'

'Take a peek yourself, then.' His sounded bemused. 'I think you'll agree that I'm one-hundred-percent correct.'

He lifted the gauze and her stomach rolled.

Imogen wandered in, her dark curls pressed to her cheek from sleep, and she clutched her emu tightly in her arms. She sidled up next to Jack. 'What are you doing?'

'I'm going to sew up Sophie's hand. Do you want to be the nurse?'

'She might want to be an assisting doctor,' Sophie snapped, challenging the stereotype that just because Imogen was a girl she'd want to be a nurse.

Jack's black brows rose. 'Point taken, but Imogen told me yesterday she wanted to be a nurse, so I thought she might like to try by holding your hand.'

Imogen smiled and grabbed Sophie's non-injured hand. 'Like this, Jack?'

'Perfect, sweetheart.'

Sophie's head started pounding. 'My medical bag is in the truck.'

'Way ahead of you there, Soph. I've got one in my room. Back in a jiff.'

'I'm helping.' Imogen squeezed her hand again, her expression desperately seeking approval.

Sophie's eczema itched. 'I really don't need you to hold my hand.'

'Of course you do.' Jack's voice brooked no argument as he returned to the kitchen and organised Sophie to sit at the table. He washed his hands, set out the suture kit and drew up local anaesthetic.

Sophie watched the methodical way he did everything, finding a reassurance in the process and trying to focus on that to keep calm.

'I got a lollipop when I got a 'jection.' Imogen continued to stand next to her, holding her hand, and pressed her leg against Sophie's thigh.

Jack grinned. 'Good idea, Im, and if Sophie's brave we'll give her one too.'

He pulled up a chair and covered Sophie's arm with a sterile drape. 'Small jab, and it will sting.'

She wanted to be anywhere but here. 'I know it will sting!'

He smiled a knowing smile. 'You're a grouchy patient, Dr Norman.'

Imogen swung around to Sophie, her small face creased in worry. 'You got to be good, Sophie, or Jack will go.'

Something inside her hurt and she tried to smile at the little girl. 'I promise I'll be good.'

Jack shot her a look that said thanks, but it was backlit with the swirling emotions of restrained anger, sadness and frustration. She remembered how angry he'd been when he told her about Imogen's mother.

He switched his attention to the little girl. 'Immy, I'm not going anywhere. I have to look after Sophie even if she's a bit grumpy, naughty or sad, and even if she cries. Just like I look after you. I'm staying right here, OK?'

Imogen nodded slowly, as if she wasn't certain she believed him, and edged even closer to Sophie so her bottom rested on her knee.

Rising panic stormed through her. She had a child on her knee and Jack touching her hand—a war zone was safer.

Jack tested the local anaesthetic with a needle. 'Can you feel that?'

Sophie shook her head, feeling woozy. 'No, it's all numb. Do your worst.'

His gaze flickered over her face. 'For you, I'll do my best.'

In that brief moment all his personas fell away—the duty-bound doctor, the foster carer, her one-time lover—and for the first time she saw the real Jack, a man of great heart. It scared her witless.

Imogen looked on fascinated as a tiny trail of black stitches marched across her hand and she peppered Jack with questions. Jack answered every one of them without the slightest trace of irritation. Sophie knew she wouldn't have had the same tolerance. Right now, the way her head was spinning, she was having trouble concentrating full-stop.

Jack finally snipped the last black thread and surveyed his handiwork. 'That should be a very neat scar as long as you keep it clean and dry this coming week.'

'A big piece of opsite should do the trick.' She sighed in relief that the stitching was over and in a moment she could make an excuse, leave the room for a few minutes and pull herself together. Jack opened up the clear, adhesive, second-skin-style dressing. 'Opsite will certainly help, but with the amount of times you have to wash your hands at work each day the best solution is for you not to work this week.'

'That's probably good advice, but who'd look after Barragong?'

He stared at her for a moment, his eyes twinkling, purple on blue, and then he leaned back and roared, laughing. 'Poor Sophie, that cut's really put you in shock. I'll work next week for you.'

Her head pounded, trying to keep track of everything. 'But you're on holidays.'

'Yeah, right.' His head inclined toward Imogen who still sat on her knee. 'I think this comes under your codicil of an emergency. We're *both* working, and next week we need to swap jobs.'

Swap jobs. Take care of Imogen. Silver spots danced in front of her eyes as the past came rushing back. *You're useless, Sophie.*

She couldn't mind the child.

Jack's eyes bored into her, his expression uncompromising. She hated that he was right about work. She'd be limited in what she could do while protecting her hand, so she really had no choice. But the fear of being home alone with Imogen made her bargain. 'We'll reassess the situation in three days.'

He shrugged as if her words hardly made an impact. 'Fair enough, but you know as well as I do you're out for a week.' He smoothed the plastic dressing over her hand, making a firm seal over the stitches, his touch totally professional. 'So, we're all done.'

Imogen shifted on her knee. 'Jack, you didn't kiss Sophie's hand better.'

He grinned at Imogen and gave her a wink. 'Well, I better fix that, then.'

Sophie went to pull her hand away. 'I really don't need—'

But his eyes darkened to navy, hypnotising her with the same need that simmered in her own veins. He raised her hand to his mouth and kissed her fingers, trailing his lips along their length with a touch so gentle and yet so erotic she thought she'd die on the spot.

Why had she ever thought coming to Australia would be safe?

* * *

'Sophie, make another one.' Imogen pushed the pile of plastic building-bricks towards her.

Sophie stifled a groan at the thought of building one more plastic tower. She looked at her watch. Five o'clock. Did that mean Jack was seeing his last patient for the day? If he was, and there was no one to check on in the hospital, he'd be home by six. She bit her lip at the irony of how she'd spent last week avoiding him, and now she wanted him here in the house as a buffer between her and Imogen.

She sighed and regrouped. She just had to get through one more hour. *Only four more working days to go.*

Jack had left her a list of suggested activities, things she might like to do with Imogen, and it had been the first list of his that she hadn't laughed at. Instead, she'd clung to it like a lifeline, and they'd done almost everything on it. The last thing was a bath.

'I think it's time to pack up and have a bath.' Sophie started to gather up the blocks.

Imogen got up and wandered over to the train set that circled the base of the Christmas tree.

Sophie stayed on the floor with the blocks and calmly tried again. 'Imogen, did you hear what I asked you to do?'

The usually compliant child squatted and turned on the train, completely ignoring Sophie. As the train chugged around the track, the tinny sound of Christmas carols blared out loudly.

A cold blast of dread ran along Sophie's spine and she took in a deep breath. 'Imogen, please turn off the train and come and help me pack up the blocks.'

Imogen clapped and sang to the train's tune.

Chris will hear the music and come home. Sophie's temple throbbed as the incessant music kept playing, and she wanted to put her hands over her ears and drown it out. With superhuman effort she held onto her composure by a thread and spoke slowly and clearly. 'Imogen, turn the train off *now*.'

The little girl didn't move but the volume of her singing increased.

Don't turn off the music, Sophie, don't touch a thing. Old memories combined with the music, all booming in her head until she couldn't stand it a moment more. She jumped to her feet and grabbed the train engine, her fingers fumbling to find the off-switch that would stop the jarring sound of the music.

'That's my train!' Imogen jumped to her feet, her small hands firmly on her hips. 'Give it back.'

Sophie's heart raced and tears pricked the back of her eyes but there was no way she could hear that train again and say in control. She placed the engine on a shelf on the sideboard. 'Imogen, it's not train time, it's bath time.' She put her free hand out towards the child. 'Let's go and make bubbles.'

'No.' Imogen stamped her foot.

'Yes.' Sophie tried placating. 'It will be fun. We can wash Sheils.'

'No.' She clutched her emu close as her voice started to rise. 'I want Jack.'

I hate you, Sophie. Her breathing started to come too fast and she fought to control it. 'Jack wants you to have a bath.'

'No.' Imogen picked up a footstool and ran to the sideboard. Climbing up, she tried to reach for the train. 'I want my train. I want my train.'

The sideboard started to wobble and Sophie swooped, grabbing Imogen around her waist and pulling her away before the child brought the heavy piece of furniture down on top of herself.

Imogen screamed, kicked and howled, her heels hammering hard into Sophie's shins. 'Go away, Sophie, go away!'

Sophie couldn't get her lungs to move any air and her fingers started to tingle as the edges of her vision blurred. *Get to safety.* She held on tightly to a squirming Imogen and somehow managed to stumble to the couch where she fell onto it, sobbing as hard as the child.

Jack hummed Christmas carols as he pulled up in front of the homestead. He'd had an enjoyable day at the clinic and when his stomach had growled at one o'clock he'd realised that the morning had flown by. Being at work was, in many ways, a lot easier than being a stay-at-home foster carer. But from about four o'clock his thoughts had strayed more and more to coming home to Imogen and Sophie, so he'd finished early, which he never did. But, then again, he was technically on holidays and the paperwork could wait.

He thought about his mother who was blissfully unaware of what was going on in their house. Although he'd shared the house with his mother since Mary had left, they lived very independent lives, and often days passed without them really seeing each other. So this last week with Sophie and Imogen in the house had been unexpectedly pleasant.

Pleasant? He grinned at the word that didn't come close to explaining the complicated house-sharing situation that had him so sexually frustrated, he was starting to have concerns for his testicles. His body hummed constantly for Sophie, and when he'd kissed her hand yesterday the only reason he hadn't trailed kisses along her arm, across her shoulder, up her neck and into her hot, lush mouth was because Imogen was in the house. But, no matter how hard it was to resist Sophie, no matter how crazy it was making him, he wasn't going to have sex with her again. He'd broken his own rule once and that had got him into this mess. He might be constantly horny but he wasn't stupid.

Yet, given all of the aggravation of his delayed holiday and living with a woman he wanted to bed so badly he could hardly see straight, he was strangely relaxed in a way he hadn't been in years—if ever. Living with Mary had been like balancing on an emotional tightrope, never quite knowing when you were going to fall off, and he had no plans ever to try and live with a woman again. But even though having Imogen and Sophie in the house was problematical it seemed to make the house buzz, something it hadn't done since he'd been a kid chasing his sisters up the hall with his father fast behind.

He hauled the esky out of the boot. He was looking forward to grilling the satay-chicken sticks he'd bought from the butcher and hearing all about Sophie and Imogen's day. As he hadn't received any text messages, he assumed all had gone well. When he'd insisted Sophie have a week off work for her hand to heal, he hadn't been totally convinced she wouldn't fight the idea. When she'd accepted without too much fuss, he'd decided that her initial stand on not wanting to mind Imogen must have stemmed from concerns about being sucked into doing everything at work and at the homestead. Given that a week ago she'd barely known him, that was understandable.

He walked down the side garden and into the courtyard. The pool shimmered blue and inviting, and he tossed around the idea of a swim after dinner. Leaving the esky next to the barbeque, he turned towards the house and saw Sophie and Imogen on the couch. Smiling, he crossed the deck and walked through the French doors, stating the obvious for no other reason than it felt damn good. 'I'm home.'

Imogen flew off the couch, her face stained with tears, and threw herself at him, sobbing.

'Hey, hey, what's wrong?' He picked her up and she immediately cuddled into his shoulder, her small chest heaving. Confused as to what had caused this uncharacteristic outburst, he glanced over her head to Sophie, seeking an answer.

She stood on unsteady legs, her eyes red-rimmed and her face white.

'Sophie?'

She shook her head and brushed past him. 'I need some air.'

Before he could speak, she'd disappeared into the garden despite the late-afternoon heat.

Two women in tears. He ran a hand through his hair, his anticipation of a quiet night at home shot to pieces. What on earth was going on?

Imogen gave a giant, shuddering sniff and rubbed her face against his shirt, her arms clinging fast around his neck. She looked utterly exhausted.

The heat was tough on everyone, especially kids, and with the excitement of Christmas around the corner it made for tired and grumpy children. 'Did you have a nap after kinder today?'

She shook her head and yawned so wide he thought she'd dislocate her jaw. 'I done swimming.' Her head stayed firm on his shoulder.

'Ah.' Heat, no nap and swimming; no wonder the kid had hit the wall and was inconsolable. She was asleep on her feet. There was no point even trying to give her dinner, she just needed her bed. He took her to the bathroom, wiped her face with a cool cloth and then tucked her into bed with the ceiling fan on low. She was asleep before he'd left the room.

He flicked off the light and closed the door. One emotional girl sorted out and one to go. He wasn't certain Sophie's problem was going to be quite so easy to fix.

CHAPTER SEVEN

JACK walked into the living area and saw the Christmas train on the top shelf of the sideboard. Imogen loved the train, but the music drove him mad so he always insisted she turn the sound off when she played with it. He picked up the engine, intending to put it back on the tracks, but something made him return it to the shelf, feeling it must be there for a reason.

Catching sight of Sophie dangling her feet in the pool, he crossed to the kitchen, made a jug of icy lemon, lime and bitters and took it out to the pool along with some tzatziki dip and biscuits. Sophie was now standing in the pool, her back to him. After setting the tray on a low table between two chairs, he grabbed Sophie's towel, walked to the end of the pool, watched and waited.

With her left arm high above her head and a plastic bag on her hand, Sophie was walking back and forth across the pool, occasionally ducking her head under to get some relief from the heat. When she finally stopped walking laps, she rose out of the water like a nymph. Water cascaded across her breasts, sluiced down her body, dividing around her belly-button ring, and then speared under the skimpy triangle of material that pretended to be her bikini bottoms. God, she was beautiful.

He wanted to pull her into his arms, feel her body mould to his and kiss her until they both gasped for air.

He handed her the towel instead. 'Feeling better?'

'Cooler.' She accepted the towel, dried her dripping hair which immediately sprang back into tight curls and then removed the plastic bag from her hand before wrapping the towel around her waist. Her shuttered eyes gave nothing away. 'Is Imogen all right?'

'She's fine and fast asleep.'

She bit her lip. 'Thanks.'

'No problem.' He ushered her to the chairs and they sat with the drinks table between them. Handing her a drink, he asked, 'Tough day?'

She sighed. 'I'm rubbish with children.'

Her words stunned him and he shook his head in instant denial. 'I've noticed you often sound like Mary Poppins when you talk to them, but the children in that book loved her.'

She traced a line in the condensation of her glass. 'Well, children don't love me.'

He frowned, wondering why she'd say this. Surely she didn't think Imogen's meltdown was personal? Yesterday Imogen had sat on Sophie's lap and happily held her hand; although Im was needy for love, she was also street smart and would avoid any adult that made her feel uncomfortable. 'Im's a pretty good judge of character, and she likes you.'

Sophie took a long gulp of her drink, her hands trembling slightly. 'Not today. She threw a tantrum of epic proportions.'

'Immy threw a tantrum?' Joy followed the surprise and he leaned back in his chair, wanting to cheer with delight. 'That's fantastic.'

Sophie's head snapped around so fast her swinging

curls released a spray of water. 'How can that possibly be a good thing?'

The sadness he always felt for Imogen rose into a rueful smile. 'Kylie hasn't given Im a very stable childhood.'

Sympathy hovered around her mouth. 'I gathered that when she told me to be good yesterday or you'd leave.'

His heart cramped at the memory. 'That's the tragedy for Imogen. She's so desperate for love and scared she'll be left, that she's normally unrealistically good. She's never a problem to look after because she's unfailingly well-behaved, but that's not normal. Kids can be right shockers, so the fact Im threw a tantrum means she's feeling safe or she's testing the waters to see if it drives us away. Either way, it's a healthy sign.'

Sophie gave a brittle laugh as her hand moved to a patch of red-raised skin on her inner elbow that looked like eczema. 'I'm glad I could be the one to trigger such an emotional breakthrough for her.'

He was pleased to hear her attempt at humour and was glad she could now see the situation in perspective, although the memory of her red-rimmed eyes and tight face lingered, generating questions. 'Believe me, she doesn't hate you. So what actually happened?'

She fiddled with the biscuits and dip before she finally spoke. 'I picked her up from kinder, we came home, had lunch and spent the afternoon working our way though your list, and we'd almost done everything—'

'My list?'

She nodded. 'The one you left for the day's activities.'

She'd used the list. Stunned disbelief spun through him. Normally she rolled her eyes and binned his Post-it notes, saying, 'You don't have to organise everything, Jack, why not live for the moment?'

'Sophie, that list was suggestions for across the week. Don't tell me you did everything on it today?'

Her tension doubled and her voice took on a sharp tone. 'Everything except the bath.'

Laughter bubbled up and he threw his head back and gave into the delicious irony. 'I'm surprised you're not as exhausted as Imogen.'

Her face, which had pinked up, paled again and her eyes flashed with anger and something else he couldn't pin down. 'I did my best, Jack. Not everyone is a natural with children like you are.'

Her agitation rocked into him, killing his laughter. What was really going on here? Who was a natural? He'd spent his life surrounded by kids and he'd learned a few tricks along the way. 'Believe me, there are some kids on some occasions that I'd cheerfully strangle—like young Lochie the day we met.'

He'd expected her to smile at the memory of their meeting but she didn't. Instead her fingers curled tightly around the edge of the towel and every part of her looked ready to flee.

I'm rubbish with children. Why would she even think like that? So she was a bit tense around kids, but that probably came from a lack of experience more than anything else, and perhaps she hadn't grown up with siblings. *The woman's worked in war zones but a healthy tantrum reduces her to tears. That's not normal.*

His brain went into overdrive trying to patch together all the pieces of the puzzle. *Imogen's your job. Children don't like me.* He suddenly remembered the train on the sideboard, neatly out of reach of the child. 'So I'm guessing that Immy spat the dummy when you confiscated the train because she was being difficult. Sounds like standard-parenting 101, and exactly what I would have done.'

'Really?' She stared at him, her eyes wide with astonishment, and it was as if she wanted to believe him but couldn't.

'Really. Imogen's tantrum was induced by tiredness and if it hadn't been the train it would have been something else. So that's Imogen's meltdown easily explained.' He leaned forward, touching her arm. 'But what brought on yours?'

Bile scalded Sophie's throat which instantly tightened as Jack's question speared straight through her heart. Her body welcomed his touch on her arm but her head screamed, *retreat*.

His eyes hooked hers, flickering with shards of blue and violet, shards of concern and care, and a determination to get an answer from her.

She gulped and spoke. 'I was tired too.'

His black brows rose in a disbelieving arch. 'You don't look tired. If anything you look totally gorgeous.' The banked desire that always simmered at the back of his eyes flared and then faded as concern returned—the concern she never wanted to see because it ate at her resolve only to think of Jack as a beautiful sex-object.

'Something really upset you, and I want to help so it doesn't happen again.'

She slipped her arm away from his touch. 'You can't wipe December from the calendar, Jack, so there's not much you can do.'

'I can listen.'

His quiet words made her ache. Pushing the straw in her glass up and down, she stared at the clinking ice. 'I'm English. We don't talk about emotions.'

He laughed. 'Well, I'm a man, and we don't talk much about them either.' His face sobered. 'But sometimes we have to, Sophie. I've seen how you flinch at loud noises, an understandable legacy from where you've been working. Did that noisy train trigger something?'

Red-hot pain rocked her. *How did he know?* It shocked her into nodding and pushed words over her lips. 'The Christmas music.'

'The reason you don't do Christmas?'

'Yes.' She sucked in a breath, knowing she'd gone past the point of no return. 'My brother vanished at Christmas when he was eleven and we never saw him again.' Steeling herself for his shocked and horrified expression, which would be followed by useless but polite platitudes, she sat stiffly and waited.

Jack slid his palm over hers, his tanned fingers interlacing with her white ones, the touch gentle but full of empathy. 'I can't imagine a family surviving something like that and making it out in one piece.'

His understanding acted like a release valve and her story came tumbling out. 'We didn't. My father was in the air force, and we'd moved every year or so, but my mother refused to leave the house we'd been living in when Chris disappeared. It became her shrine to his memory. If we could pretend for most of the year that a part of her hadn't died when Chris disappeared, we had no hope at Christmas. The third Christmas after he vanished Mum had a psychotic episode, and Dad had the horrendous task of putting his wife into care so he could try and save the rest of us.'

'That would have to be one of the hardest things a man could do.' Compassion wove through his words. 'How many other siblings do you have?

She thought of her sisters. 'We're three girls and all

of us are flung out across the world. I'm the eldest, then there's Amelia, who's a pilot in the air force just like Dad. She's currently based in Germany and my youngest sister, Minty, is nineteen and reading literature at Oxford.'

His wondrous smile washed over her. 'A talented group of women.'

'Thanks.' The cosy warmth that rolled through her was disproportionate to the compliment and she tried to shake it away, but it stuck to her ribs. 'Dad was a stickler for education, and when Mum was so sick Emmy and I clung to school as the one thing in our lives that was dependable and unchanging.'

'Minty must have been very young when all this happened.'

'She was four when Dad became a sole parent, and I was fourteen.'

His handsome face saw too much. 'A lot can be expected of the eldest child.'

The memories of raising Minty flooded back. 'Dad did his best but there was no other way. We'd lost our brother and our mother, but we had to honour their lives by surviving and filling our lives with achievements. For three years I went to classes, cared for my sisters and somehow managed to keep up with my school work.'

'That's tough.'

She didn't want his sympathy and she tugged her hand out of his. 'It was probably a really good thing, because it taught me that I wasn't cut out to be a mother.'

Shock crossed his face. 'Cut yourself some slack, Sophie. You were a kid raising a kid. Parenting is the hardest job an adult ever faces, and even then not everyone manages it.'

She knew he was thinking of Imogen's mother but she

didn't want his understanding or to hear his philosophy on parenting. 'Amelia was fourteen when I went to university and she did a much better job with Minty than I'd done at the same age.'

Two deep lines carved into his forehead. 'Have you ever considered the fact that Minty was seven when Amelia took over? That by then Minty was in the concrete stage of development? That's the easiest time for parenting. It's the calm before the puberty storm.' His intelligent eyes swept her face. 'Who looked after her for the tricky adolescent years?'

'My father.'

'How'd he do?'

She thought about her father's emails during that time, about his despair at Minty's constant rebellious partying, how he hadn't been able to understand why she was socialising with a wild crowd that she ran rings around intellectually. All Sophie had been able to do was be thankful she didn't have to deal with it. It had taken a bad car accident to jolt her sister into maturity. The mostly hard-working university student of today with a flair for fun was a far cry from the traumatised girl of fourteen.

Jack filled the silence. 'He found it damn hard, right? And he was what, fifty-something?'

His words fell like mortar fire and she wanted to hide her head under her arms and duck for cover. But anger kept her in the chair. 'What is it about men who presume to tell me what I should and shouldn't want?' The moment she'd spoken, she wanted to grab back the words but it was too late. She saw the second that Jack's quick mind made the connection.

'Was this the reason you and Simon broke up?'

There was no point denying it. 'Yes. He wanted children and I didn't.'

He spoke softly. 'That must have been tough on both of you.'

Couples who love each other make a family, Sophie. She forced Simon's cajoling voice out of her head and, with a jaw so tight it ached, she forced out her words. 'The relationship had run its course, and I don't have a problem with my decision not to have children.'

He raised his brows. 'Even if it's based on an illogical rationale?'

'Don't you dare tell me it's illogical. You weren't there living the mess that was half my childhood. At least I have enough insight to know where my strengths lie, and I'm not going to bring a child into the world that I'd only end up traumatising.'

He shrugged as if he disagreed but then his fingers, cool and soothing, traced the patch of eczema on her arm. 'I think it's a shame you think this way, because if you just relaxed a bit you'd be great with children.'

She wanted to let his words roll off her because she knew herself a hell of a lot better than a man who'd only known her just over a week. She knew she didn't want children. It had to be true because she'd hurt Simon so badly by not loving him and not wanting his child. But Jack's words lingered, settling over her like a fine mist and seeping into her.

Her heart rate picked up as fear trickled through her. *Change the topic now!* 'It sounds like you want kids of your own, Jack.'

'Maybe one day, but right now I can't see past my trip.'

'Still, after the trip, if you decided that you wanted

to settle down and start a family that would involve a relationship, right?'

He tensed, his eyes wary. 'What are you getting at, Sophie?'

The goddess woke up and saw a chance to talk about sex and touch base with the bad boy, hopefully bringing him out to play. Sophie smiled, loving the flirting rush. 'Well, you have to have sex to make a baby, Jack—and isn't your insane "no sex in Barragong" rule going to make conceiving a tad tricky?'

His stunned expression was like that of a deer caught in headlights as he processed the fact that the situation had just changed. He shot to his feet. 'Don't go there, Sophie. We've talked about why we can't have sex again.'

'Because you believe you have to be an upstanding citizen.' She stood up; her towel fell from her waist and right on cue, his gaze fell to her hips. She stepped in close, her breasts mere millimetres away from his chest, gazed up into his eyes and spoke softly. 'I think your reasons are based on an illogical rationale.'

'No. They're. Not.' He ground out the words but he didn't move away from her, and raging need burned in his eyes.

'I don't want a relationship, Jack, and unlike your ex-wife I'm not going to tell you that you have to choose me or the town because I'll be moving on the moment my contract finishes. But here's the thing that I do want from you—December is really hard for me and I'm struggling in this Christmas-infested house. Sex with you would really help me out.'

A pulse bulged in his neck. 'Sex is your stress management?'

She nodded, realising with a start that he was spot

on with his assessment. 'Uncomplicated sex can be cathartic, Jack. It has to be better than the tension we've been living with this last week, trying to ignore the fact we both want to tear each other's clothes off every time we see each other.'

He jerked as if hit by an electric shock and then his mouth took hers, hard, fast and gloriously wicked. Her Jack was back. She gripped his shirt as her bones melted and she closed her eyes, wanting to block out everything except his wondrous touch and taste. He tasted of heat, of repressed need, of thundering and earthy lust, and she sucked it all in like a parched tree in the desert.

His fingers trailed across the thin Lycra of her bikini top and her nipples pebbled into hard, aching nubs desperate for the touch of his mouth. The strain of the last week fell away and nothing existed except his mouth on hers. She spun out on a stream of bliss as sensation upon sensation built inside her, sending her soaring towards the promise of ecstasy. Her head fell back and she heard herself moaning as his mouth trailed down her neck to the soft skin of her breasts. Heat pooled between her legs as he pressed himself against her, his arousal matching her own.

As his hands cupped her buttocks and she prepared to be lifted off the ground so she could wrap her legs around his waist, she doubted they'd make it to either one of their bedrooms. He suddenly pulled back and her eyes snapped open.

His chest heaved raggedly and a duel raged deep in the navy of his eyes: wildness and restraint. Need and duty. Longing and denial. His hands gripped her upper arm and his voice, raspy and hoarse, scratched her skin. 'There have to be rules.'

Her heart spasmed and her desire died. This wasn't

the Jack she wanted. The Jack she'd met on that first day wouldn't have had rules. He would have taken her offer and taken her right by the pool. But this was the constrained and caged Jack, and she wanted to shake him. She didn't want rules, she didn't want sensible, she just wanted to lose herself in him, live for the moment and forget.

Blinking back tears of disappointment, she stepped out of his grip. 'Rules are for wimps, Jack.'

His eyes flashed royal purple. 'That's rich coming from someone who's hiding behind sex.'

The arrow struck her with uncanny accuracy. 'And you're hiding from the life you want.' She scooped up her towel and somehow managed to force her unsteady legs to carry her to her room.

Jack fell back into the chair, shaking as Sophie slammed the door to the east wing behind her. She'd offered him straightforward sex, no strings attached, but instead of taking it at face value, no questions asked, he'd tried to control her offer. He ran his hands through his hair. What the hell was wrong with him? His body called for hers constantly; it only took one whiff of her perfume and he was hard and fantasising. It had taken every ounce of his self-control, and then some, not to pull her down into this chair and take her on his lap.

She'd called him a wimp but there was no way in the world a wimp could have walked away from her offer. His request for rules was to protect Imogen. She needed stability.

The Armitages see the big picture, Jack. We're blessed with money and position and it's our responsibility to care. His father's voice floated through him. 'Hell, Dad, the price is getting pretty steep.'

Was he hiding from life? He poured himself another

cool drink, envying Sophie the freedom she had in her life, the way she just went for what she wanted and roved the world, working and grasping life with both hands.

She's doing that because she's running.

With a shaft of utter clarity, he suddenly realised that perhaps the freedom he was so envious of wasn't really freedom at all. He wanted a break from Barragong—hell, he needed a long and relaxing break—but he wasn't certain he wanted to leave forever. Sophie hadn't been home in years and that in itself meant her perceived freedom to go anywhere she wished was a falsehood. He grimaced as he pictured her cutting response to *that* thought if he ever floated it past her.

I'm struggling in this Christmas-infested house. Her obvious desire for him hadn't been enough to mask the pleading in her eyes. She wanted to use him to get through December. He scratched his jaw, the end-of-the-day stubble rough under his fingertips. He sensed she'd accepted her brother's probable death and had got on with her life—she wouldn't have qualified as a doctor otherwise—but he acknowledged the association of the festive season with all the ensuing unhappiness, would make December a really tough month.

He sighed and slumped in the chair. He had two females in his home who really needed a positive and happy Christmas experience, but for two very different reasons. Exactly how he was going to achieve that was the big question.

Sophie peered at the list of reports she'd accessed online from the Flinders Medical Centre pathology department and made notes. When she'd come back from her early-morning run, Jack had greeted her with a smile. She hadn't expected that. Usually calling a man a wimp meant he really didn't want to talk to you much after that. But Jack being Jack had confounded her yet again by not taking the expected path, and had added to the surprise by making her breakfast. Then he'd insisted she come to into work while Imogen was at kinder.

'You're on paperwork only, and you can take the medical phone queries which will free up nursing time.'

But his expression had been loaded with understanding and her heart had quivered. He knew being in the decorated house on her own was tough for her and that coming to work would keep her busy.

'Anything we should know about, Sophie?'

The words brought her back to the here and now and she spun her chair around to Diana, who was standing behind her looking weary and rubbing her lower back.

'Mr Rowan's blood cultures haven't grown anything so it looks like the fever's viral. I'm still waiting for his liver-function test results.'

Diana blew out a breath. 'OK, so no changes to treatment at the moment?'

Sophie nodded her agreement. 'But you're looking worn out. Should you even be here with the baby so close?'

Diana gave what Sophie was learning was the laconic Australian shrug. 'Jenny Palmer's child is sick and Geoff's out mustering, so she needs to be at home. It's a crazy time of year and hard to get staff at short notice, so here I am.'

'Anything I can do to help?'

Diana hesitated.

'Really, I'm happy to do anything that doesn't involve bodily fluids because of this hand.'

The nurse looked uncertain. 'Would you mind doing the morning drug-round?'

'No problem.'

'What's no problem?' Jack's genuine smile raced through dark stubble, curved around his dimple and sparkled in his eyes which were fixed on Diana.

A green flash of jealousy ripped through Sophie so hard it hurt. She'd seen him smile at Imogen like that, and now at Diana, but not at her. Since Parachilna his smiles for her were tight and so filled with tension they almost cracked.

'Sophie's doing the drug round for me.' A patient buzzer sounded at the desk and Diana hurried off to answer it.

He leaned over the counter, staring down at her. 'Will you have that done by noon?'

She wanted to reach up and bury her hands in his hair but she reminded herself that her desire was for the physical Jack and not this man of duty. 'Yes.' She gritted her teeth. 'You don't have a monopoly on duty, Jack. I don't break my promises, and I know I'm collecting Imogen from kinder at twelve-fifteen p.m.'

'Actually, that wasn't why I was asking.'

His quietly spoken words added to her already jumbled and contrary emotions, and she wanted to scream. It should have been so simple: just sex. Jack wanted her. She wanted him. But he'd changed into someone she feared on a visceral level and knew she needed to avoid—the caring man who deserved a family. The type of man she didn't want to like because the risk of hurting him was just too high. She'd learned from Simon, which was why she'd tried so hard to tempt the bad boy back out again so she could feel safe. But just lately, when he looked at her as he was doing right now, she felt her resolve against the nice guy slipping.

She breathed in deeply. 'What do you want me to do at noon?'

He gave her a mysterious smile. 'I'll meet you here. By the way, have you got an update on Lara's pathology?'

Glad to be back on safe territory, she moved the mouse over Lara's name and brought up the file. 'Do you remember how she'd had symptoms of Giardia or some other parasitic infection? Well, it turns out it was Crohn's disease.'

A contemplative expression crossed Jack's face. 'And, undiagnosed and untreated, it perforated her bowel. She was damn lucky we were in Parachilna that night.'

She smiled up at him in total agreement. 'It was a good save. We do good work, Jack, and we're appreciated.' She wondered if part of his love-hate relationship with the town was due to feeling under-appreciated, or whether he was just frustrated by the delay in his trip. She pushed an envelope towards him. 'We got a lovely letter and card from Lara and Paul in today's post, thanking us for all we did.'

'That was kind of them.' He pocketed the letter and gave her a wave. 'Clinic calls; back at noon.'

Sophie gave a weak smile and stood up to start the drug round, thankful she had patients to talk to who'd keep her mind off what Jack had planned.

CHAPTER EIGHT

AT FIVE-PAST noon Imogen rode into the hospital on Jack's shoulders, her eyes shining, waving a piece of paper like it was a flag. 'Sophie, Sophie, guess what?'

The child's enthusiasm was hard to resist and Sophie smiled. 'I don't think I could possibly guess.'

'I'm the emu in the 'tivity play at kinder.'

'The emu?' She shot Jack a confused look. 'They had an emu at the birth of Jesus?'

He winked. 'Absolutely. Along with three wise wombats, two kangaroos, a baby joey and a few scurrying bilbies.'

His warmth and humour washed through her and she hugged it close. *Let it go; not wise.* 'An emu—OK, then, obviously I'm not up to speed with things.' She smiled up at the little girl. 'That's brilliant news, Imogen.'

Imogen grinned. 'And, Sophie, I gotta wear a costume and bring a plate of biccies, and Jack said we could make gingerbread men with lolly buttons.'

Sophie's chest tightened as she caught Jack's eye. 'We?'

A sheepish grin played across his lips and he jangled his keys as if to say, 'walk and talk'.

They headed out the door, the trip to the car hot and slow as Imogen excitedly told everyone she met about the kinder concert. Jack strapped Imogen into her car seat, put headphones over her ears and pressed start on a talking book. She immediately started singing along to the opening music.

He swung up into the driver's seat, his body filling the seat and his aura filling the car. His arm landed on the back of her headrest as he reversed out of the car park. 'Next stop, home.'

Her head started to tilt towards his arm as everything about him—his scent of sunshine and work, his sparkling eyes, golden skin and his unexpectedly relaxed attitude—called to her.

It's not your home; you don't want one, remember? She straightened up, snapped her seat belt in place and shot him a questioning look. 'Let's go back to the "we", Jack.'

His sheepish expression returned with a plea-bargaining edge. 'Here's the thing, Soph. I can follow a recipe and make a fair attempt at gingerbread, but I can't sew.'

She scoffed. 'You sewed up my hand beautifully.'

Apprehension crawled along his cheeks. 'Put it this way, then, I have no clue about an emu costume.'

Panic skittered through her. 'And you think I do? I'm English!'

'So what are we going to do?' His voice rose uncharacteristically. 'Last year Kylie took off in early December with Im and she missed out on being part of the concert, so it's really important that she takes part this year. I know the kinder teacher says keep it simple, but I also know there are mothers out there who've spent the last month making their kid a costume. Her costume has to be equal to theirs because I won't have Im feeling like she doesn't belong.'

His knuckles whitened on the steering wheel as tension rolled back in and he glanced at her, his eyes filled with such care and gallantry that Sophie had to stifle a gasp. She wondered what it would feel like to be the focus of such attention.

She bit her lip, holding the memories of Minty at bay, because she wanted to help but she felt totally clueless. 'I don't even know where to start.'

He groaned. 'I know what you mean. This is where we need Mum. She'd just go into the cupboard under the stairs, rustle around a bit and come out with the perfect thing.'

'There's a cupboard under the stairs?' Sophie sat up a bit higher in the seat and tossed her curls back off her face. 'I guess we start there, then.'

An hour later, Sophie emerged from the treasure trove that was the 'cupboard' under the stairs, although it was really more like a small room complete with a sewing table. She walked into the sunroom, her hands behind her back. 'Hey, Imogen, where's Sheils?'

The little girl slipped off the high kitchen stool where she'd been 'helping' Jack bake and picked up the abandoned toy bird from the couch. 'Here she is.'

Sophie glanced at the toy and couldn't help smiling at her perfect find. 'Close your eyes, Imogen.'

'Why?'

Sophie breathed in slowly. 'You'll see.'

Imogen stared at her for a long moment, and a trickle of unease bubbled along Sophie's veins, but then the little girl closed her eyes.

Sophie knelt down so they were both at head height and wrapped a bright feather boa around Imogen's neck, the exact vivid blue of the toy emu's neck. 'You can open them now.'

Imogen did as she was told and when she saw the boa her eye's widened into pools of wonder. 'I got a blue neck too.' She shot forward, her body slamming into Sophie's chest and her small arms looping around her neck in a full-on body hug.

Sophie nearly toppled backwards and she wrapped her arms around the little girl to steady herself. Imogen's body stayed snuggled in against her own, warm, trusting and giving, and Sophie hugged her back.

Deep down inside her, something moved.

But children aren't your thing. Stunned and disoriented at the odd sensation that had come and gone so quickly that she wondered if she'd imagined it, she extricated herself from the child. 'I'm glad you like it.' She stood up, brushing blue feathers off her shorts and walked into the kitchen, pressing a glass against the cold-water dispenser of the fridge. She drained it in one gulp.

'That's a great idea, Soph, thanks.'

She turned to meet Jack's all-seeing eyes and smiling face, complete with flour on his cheeks, and her insides rolled again, only this time she recognised the emotion—lust—pure but, oh, so not simple. 'It's a start, and I know what we'll be doing tonight.'

His brows rose as if he was going to warn her again about not bringing up the topic of sex but he didn't say a word.

She tilted her chin. 'It involves feathers, a leotard, cardboard and a glue-gun.'

His eyes darkened to deep purple and his lips twitched. 'Sounds kinky.'

The glass nearly slipped out of her hand. Jack had just made a joke, the first one since he'd left for Parachilna, and a delicious warmth rolled through her. She laughed and spun past him, loving the gleam in his eye. 'That depends entirely on where you put the feathers.'

He threw his head back and laughed.

'I want to make the lolly buttons.' Imogen clambered up onto the stool, still wearing the boa, and with Sheils tucked under her arm.

Jack's laughter lines morphed into a *faux* serious expression. 'Sorry, but I don't think emus eat lollies or make gingerbread men.'

'It's just me, Jack, and I'm a girl.'

He scratched his chin. 'Are you? You've got a blue neck, which means you're an emu.' He pressed the cookie cutter into the fragrant dough.

Imogen quickly took off the boa. 'Look, I a girl like you, aren't I, Sophie?'

The itch of her eczema faded slightly and she nodded. 'You're a girl, just like me. Let's put three sweets on the gingerbread man's tummy and one in our mouths.' A streak of lightness raced through her as she grabbed a handful of chocolate buttons, dropped them in her mouth and laughed.

Jack wanted to cheer. For the first time he saw real happiness in Sophie's eyes and he wanted to pull her against him and kiss her until they fell onto the kitchen bench and explored each other's bodies from top to toe, with or without chocolate sauce from the fridge. But he was wearing an apron, covered in flour and had a five-year-old girl in front of him wanting to cook. 'Hey, Im, are we going to let Sophie get away with stealing all the lollies?'

'Sweets.' Imogen corrected him, using the English word and trying to sound like Sophie.

He laughed. 'Sweets or lollies, honey, she's eating way too many of them.'

'I promise I'll be good.' Sophie's eyes danced and her fingers darted towards the bowl.

'Im, it's tickle time.'

'Oh, no.' Sophie dodged out from the kitchen bench and into the sunroom.

'Get her, Jack.'

Jack grabbed Sophie around the waist as Imogen hopped off the chair and threw herself at Sophie with a rugby tackle around the knees. Fingers tickled under arms, around waists and behind knees, and laughter rained over them all until, exhausted, the three of them fell onto the couch.

Sophie ended up across Jack's chest and Imogen sat on top of Sophie. Sophie's weight against his body reminded him of the day they'd met. The scent of her hair brought back the memory of how amazing it had been to bury his face in it, and her laughing lips taunted him that they could be his again if he chose. She reminded him of everything he'd given up.

You're hiding from the life you want, Jack.

'I surrender.' Sophie gasped, struggled to sit up, and fell back.

Imogen crossed her arms and stared down at her. 'What does that mean?'

Jack smiled. 'It means Sophie is going to be a good girl and do what we tell her.'

'I don't know about that.' Sophie tilted her chin back so her eyes met his and he recognised the need burning there as hot as his own.

I don't want a relationship, Jack, I just want sex.

There's more than one solution to every problem, son.

Jack couldn't believe he'd been so stupid.

Sophie managed to sit up and she lifted Imogen off

her lap. Rising to her feet, she tried to tuck her curls behind her ears, but it was a hopeless task and she gave up. Instead, she put her hand out to Imogen. 'Let's get back to work, shall we? Those gingerbread men might run away if we leave them alone for too long.'

This time the British nanny sounded a lot more relaxed, and Jack smiled.

Sophie sat on the couch with her laptop, reading an email from her father filled with hints about her coming home for a visit, when she suddenly realised the house was uncharacteristically quiet. She glanced towards the corner of the sunroom where less than three minutes ago Imogen had been drawing at her little table. She wasn't there.

'Imogen.' Sophie hurriedly pushed back her chair, and started walking down the hall towards the bedrooms. 'Imogen?' The room was empty.

She noticed that the door to Jack's mother's room was open and she walked in. 'Imogen?'

'I hiding here.' The little girl's voice was muffled.

Sophie opened the door to the *en suite* but it was empty. Puzzled, she called out again. 'Imogen, where are you?'

'It's hidey. You have to find me.'

Sophie smiled at the five-year-old's version of the game where she'd forgotten to tell the seeker they were playing. 'I wonder where you can be?' A moment later she heard a giggle.

She checked under the bed but all she could see were neatly wrapped Christmas gifts. Perhaps Jack got his organisational skills from Min. 'You're not under the bed.'

Another giggle. 'I know.'

The only other place left was the enormous wardrobe with its intricate carving. Surely she wasn't in there? She put her ear against the door and said, 'I'm coming to get you.'

She heard more muffled giggles.

Opening the latch, she pulled open the door. It was filled with beautiful clothes and boxes of shoes, and it was hard to imagine Imogen could possibly be inside. She peered under the clothes into the darkness and stretched out her hand, expecting to hit the back of the wardrobe, but she only touched space. She moved out some shoe boxes and crawled in.

As her eyes adjusted to the dim light she made out Imogen sitting in the far corner and cuddling Sheils. She reached out towards her. 'Gotcha!'

Imogen squealed with delight and sat in her lap. 'Look, Sophie, Min has a light.'

Sophie saw an old-fashioned pull-cord light and she reached up and turned it on. They sat surrounded by shoes and clothes and hats. 'This is amazing.'

'I like to play here.' Imogen rested her head against Sophie's shoulder. 'Tell me the story about Christmas when you were a little girl.'

The familiar ache that always bored through Sophie when she thought of Christmas rose inside her, but she pushed past it, thinking instead of the Christmas in Surrey spent in a rambling house not dissimilar to this one. She remembered the glowing, open fires, a fresh pine-tree, snow on the ground, playing hide and seek inside the house with Chris and her sisters, and skating on the pond on Christmas afternoon. The memory made her smile. 'When I was a little girl, a bit older than you, my brother and sisters and I built a snow man.'

'Tell me another Christmas story.'

'My mother used to make plum puddings and hang them in the attic.' Sophie leaned back against the back of the deep wardrobe and settled in for a story-telling session, because if she'd learned anything in a week it was that Imogen had an inexhaustible amount of questions.

'Dr Armitage, we've located Kylie in Tamworth.' The voice of Carmel the social worker came down the line.

His anger bubbled out. 'What guitar-playing country singer did she chase there this year?'

Carmel ignored his rhetorical question. 'She said she's interested in pursuing a career as a country and western singer and she's agreed to permanent care for Imogen.'

He grunted. 'She has this week, anyway.' Kylie had a history of changing her mind. He remembered the night he'd delivered the bright-eyed Imogen into the world, and the days following when Kylie had toyed with the idea of giving Im up for adoption, before changing her mind at the last minute and thus setting up the roller-coaster that was the little girl's life.

'No, Jack, we were very clear on what that meant. We offered her extra help and support if she returned to Barragong but she isn't interested in being a parent any more. The only thing she was quite specific about was that she wants you and Min to raise her child.'

'Respite care is one thing, Carmel, but permanent care is a huge deal.' Jack rubbed the back of his neck, feeling trapped. 'I can't make any decisions until my mother gets back, especially as I'm heading off on long-service leave for a few months.'

'I know it's a big decision, Jack. Permanent care means you become a father with all the inherent joys and heartaches that role brings. But being a father is a very special thing, and all I'm asking is that you give it due consideration before you reject it out of hand. I'll be in touch.'

The line went dead.

Jack's head hammered so hard it felt like it would explode from the tension. Imogen needed a family—she deserved that. He had a trip to take—he was owed that. Hell, he'd given it up twice already, and he didn't want to do it again. The walls of the house pressed in on him, echoing with voices of the past until he thought he'd go mad. He couldn't stay here any longer. He grabbed his keys and headed out the door.

Sophie tore off the latex gloves and dropped them in the treatment room's bin, loving the fact her stitches had come out an hour ago. Diana had removed them and thus ended the incessant itching that had been with her for the last few days. The neat, red line now had a clear plaster over it just for added protection but the cut had healed beautifully. Jack's handiwork was faultless. It felt great to be doing hands-on medicine again. She felt great. She hadn't experienced such a relaxed December since she'd been eleven.

She smiled at her patient. 'Mrs Stephenson, this ulcer is really nasty and it needs a daily dressing. I'm sure between myself and the nurses we can arrange something so you don't have to tramp in here every day.'

'You're a sweet girl, dear, thank you.' The elderly patient patted Sophie's hand. 'I bet you're finding Barragong a lot hotter than grey, old England.'

Sophie laughed. 'It does seem odd not to have snow and cold weather in December, but I think I prefer your sunshine.' She'd been mulling over her calm state. Granted, she'd noticed Jack had removed every second

Christmas ornament from the stationary surfaces in the house, but she really thought the weather made a huge difference to her well-being.

You go right ahead and think that in your deluded little world. Jack's the difference.

No way, no way, not possible at all.

'Right, then, let's get you back to your husband.' Sophie grabbed at the wheelchair handles and started walking quickly, wanting to escape the argument in her head.

Mrs Stephenson giggled like a girl. 'Steady there, doctor, there isn't a fire.'

'Sorry, I'll slow down—' But she stopped dead.

Jack stood at the nurses' station in black leather trousers and a white T-shirt. He turned and smiled, all wicked charm and bad-boy intent.

A fast rush of heat whooshed through her body, liquefying every cell, and her grip on the wheelchair handles was the only thing keeping her upright.

Mrs Stephenson sighed and gave Jack a wave as she leaned back to Sophie. 'That young man is a wonderful doctor, and *very* easy on the eyes.'

Sophie's tight throat only managed a squeak in reply. Was the Jack she wanted so badly really back?

Jack strode over, concern and conscientiousness clear on his handsome face.

Her stomach rolled in disappointment. Perhaps he wasn't back after all.

He squatted in front of the wheelchair. 'Elsie, what happened to your leg?'

'Now, Jack, don't fuss. Sophie here has me all sorted out, and it might have taken me fifty-five years but I have David well trained to cook and clean.'

Mr Stephenson stepped up, a large and benevolent

smile on his face. 'Don't listen to a word, Jack. I taught her everything she knows.'

Jack stood up, laughing, and shook David's hand. 'Sophie, David and my father threw legendary barbeques that could only be described as gourmet.'

David nodded and Sophie knew both men were thinking of Dr Armitage senior who for that moment seemed to be in the room with them. In the last couple of weeks, she'd often thought he was visiting with Jack.

David covered his wife's hand. 'Ready to go, love?'

Elsie gave a long sigh. 'Yes, and I'm looking forward to one of your lovely cups of tea. Everyone here tries, but they can't make one as well as you.'

Diana waddled over with a large plastic bag full of dressing packs. 'Elsie, we've got a roster going, so if you have your shower at nine and then lie on the bed with the ulcer open to the air one of us will be there at ten each day.'

Elsie accepted the large bag, placed it on her lap and glanced at everyone. 'Will I be able to go to Carols by Candlelight on Christmas Eve? My granddaughter's in the nativity play and I've made her wombat costume. I *really* want to see her in it.'

Jack grinned. 'Well, as a fellow costume maker…'

'Excuse me?' Sophie gave a snort. 'If I remember correctly, I was the one who got covered in feathers and battled the temperamental glue-gun.'

Jack smiled sagely and spoke directly to Elsie. 'I made the tea.'

Elsie patted his arm and then beamed up at Sophie. 'A good man knows when to hang back, dear, and when to step up. Tea is probably what you needed.'

Sophie remembered how stressed she'd been with the costume and how Jack had removed the sticky mess from her lap, sat down next to her and passed her a cup of fragrant Earl Grey tea. The shifting sensation she'd experienced on and off in the last two weeks tilted again, sending dangerous waves of longing and belonging through her.

Don't be ridiculous, you didn't need tea. You need and want what Jack won't give—uncomplicated sex.

Sophie glanced at her watch. 'Diana, can you please escort David and Elsie out to the car? Otherwise I'll be late for kinder pick-up and Imogen gets anxious.'

'No problem.' The nurse ushered the Stephensons towards the front door.

Jack stayed put.

She bit her lip and gave him a long look, not certain what was going on, but being a lot more cautious than she'd been the first day she'd met him when she'd missed all the signs that he was a sheep in wolf's clothing. God, he was gorgeous. And untouchable. Rather than put herself through the agonies of wanting, she headed towards the other exit. He easily fell into step beside her and she could feel his gaze lazily drifting over her.

She spoke briskly. 'I'm glad you went for a ride.'

'I made a different choice.'

His words were her words coming back to her—words she thought he hadn't even heard. She walked outside, the heat hitting her like a fist. 'That's great, but why are you here now? I thought you were doing afternoon clinic today, and it doesn't start until two.'

His eyes sparkled with swirls of violet and blue. 'You're right, it doesn't, but I came to get you.'

Her heart picked up only to plummet again. 'I have to collect Imogen.'

He slid his hand along her palm, his fingers wrapping around hers. 'Imogen's on a play date.'

Her heart hammered so loudly she could hardly hear her own words. 'A play date? What's that?'

'It means she's at the Dempseys' house playing with Lochie until you collect her at two.' He leaned in close, his eyes hungry for her and his words heavy with need. 'We have two hours where no one needs us.'

'No one needs us?' Her brain turned to sludge as her blood sped through her body, firing off every pleasure point and making them hum with vibrating need. She tried hard to hold onto common sense and control but the goddess had already slipped into something more comfortable. For two weeks Jack had been determined not to have sex in Barragong and now suddenly the bad boy was back. It didn't make sense.

Does it matter why?

'Sophie.' Jack's eyes bored into her and her name came out on a moan.

All thoughts vanished. 'If we have two hours to ourselves, why are we standing here?'

His eyes flared with heat and his lips pressed against hers in a kiss so hot, hard and fast it sucked the breath from her lungs.

He pulled back. 'You're right, we're wasting time.' Striding out, he tugged her behind him, and ten paces later they stood next to the silver-and-black motorcycle that was glinting in the sunshine. He tossed her a helmet, swung his legs over the bike and a moment later the engine roared to life. He turned towards her and smiled.

Oh, yes. Her Jack was back. She swung up behind him, wrapped her arms around him and let the breadth of his back and the heat of his body flood into her. She breathed in the scent of leather, sweat and sunshine as her legs contoured to his and her head rested on his shoulder. She'd longed to touch him for so long and she soaked him up like a dry sponge absorbing water, feeling her body opening up and expanding in a way it never had before.

The bike tore down the familiar road, taking the turn at the yellow forty-four-gallon drum, and the homestead came into sight. Anticipation of tumbling into bed with Jack almost made her lose her balance but he didn't cross the cattle grid into the drive. Instead he turned left and jolted down a rocky dirt-red track.

Simmering anticipation turned to abject frustration. What was he doing? They had two hours, so why was he wasting time? The bike turned again, this time away from the rocky, grassless plains and down a steep incline until the road flattened out again. Majestic river red-gums, gnarly and scarred, some with trunks the width of a small car, lined a dry, rocky creek bed, and behind them the sheer cliffs of a gorge towered above. The red, brown and yellow colours of the rocks contrasted dramatically against the eucalypt, green leaves and white bark. It was hot, harsh and one of the most vividly beautiful places she'd ever seen.

Jack stopped the bike. He swung off, removed his helmet and rummaged around in the panniers. Then he stripped off his leathers.

Sophie's questions about what Jack had planned stalled as she was deliciously sidetracked by watching his long, muscular legs appear. The questions resumed when he pulled on a pair of shorts. 'Why are we here, Jack?'

He gave her a smile that only generated more questions than it answered. 'Trust me, Soph.'

She realised with a start that she did. She trusted him absolutely.

Pulling out a small day-pack from the panniers, he held out a crumpled sun-hat. 'Put this on and the adventure begins.'

She jammed it on her head, then his hand grabbed hers and they walked further along the creek bed. The need to talk vanished and the only sounds she could hear were the clink of the rocks under her feet, the occasional squawk of a black cockatoo and the sound of her breathing.

Jack suddenly stopped, and with his arm around her shoulder he pointed up high on the cliff wall and whispered, 'Yellow-footed rock wallaby.'

She squinted and then gasped in delight as she saw in the dark shadows of a cliff ledge a small wallaby with a grey body, yellow-furred legs and a beautiful black-and-yellow-striped tail. 'That's amazing.'

He grinned and started walking again, and soon turned left, heading into a narrower part of the gorge. The rocks underfoot became damp, and occasional puddles of water appeared. They started climbing up massive rocks that had been smoothed by millions of years of water rushing over them at various times.

Jack scaled the rocks with the expertise of someone who'd done this climb many times before, and as he advanced each level he kneeled down, extended his arm and hauled Sophie upwards. She gripped his hand, needing his help to scramble up, and loving the chance to touch him.

Water seeped through the rocks and unlike lower down, where the cliffs were bare, vegetation clung to the sheer faces. She could see trees growing out of the rocks and she wondered how they clung there with scant soil to hold them in place. She took a moment to catch her breath and looked up. High above her a wedge-tail eagle circled, looking for lunch from an unsuspecting snake sunning itself in the sunshine.

'Almost there, Soph.' Jack reached down again. 'Put your foot there and there.' He pointed to two natural footholds.

She did as instructed and the next minute he'd lifted her the last metre and she stood beside a large and sparkling water-hole carved deep in the vivid, red rocks.

'What do you think?' Jack's expression was one of pride and boyish eagerness.

'This country is amazing. I can't believe there's a water hole here and lush vegetation when everything that surrounds it's so dry.'

He grinned. 'The desert's got its secrets and this is one of them.' He unlaced his boots, hauled his T-shirt over his head, dropped his shorts, kicked off his boxers and dived in.

Sophie didn't move. Her gaze was fixed on his lean and muscular body streaking through the clear water.

He surfaced, water streaming over his face. 'Stop ogling and come join me.'

She didn't need a second invitation. Fumbling with her boots, she finally managed to pull them off. Fortunately, her loose Indian clothing came off easily and with a shout of pure joy she jumped in. As she kicked up from the surprisingly cold depths into the warm surface-water, hands circled her waist and she was pulled onto a ledge and into Jack's arms.

She stared up at him, hardly able to believe she was in this beautiful place and alone with Jack. She didn't ask him why he'd changed his mind about having sex because all she cared about was that he had. 'This is divine.'

He shook his head. 'No, this is.'

His lips met hers but not in the hard and heady rush of need she knew from his previous kisses. This time his touch was satiny soft and he explored her lips in a slow and languid trail, each caress firing her with desperate need that built inside her until she thought she'd scream.

She opened her mouth under his, wanting to throw herself into the frenzy that had been their last coupling, but Jack continued exploring her bottom lip as if it was the only part of her that existed. She gripped his shoulders in frustration.

He raised his head, his smile a mixture of playfulness and understanding. 'There's no hurry, Sophie. We're in a beautiful place, you're a beautiful woman and I intend to take my time.'

She sighed, disappointment ramming her hard, and she was left wondering why they couldn't have just gone to the homestead. 'The cold water got to you, didn't it?'

He laughed and pulled her across his lap, his arousal hard against her thigh. 'It's not a problem at all. You, on the other hand, just need to relax.'

Relax? Was he insane? She'd wanted him so badly for so long that this was a form of torture. The sex they had together was high octane and fast: that was what she knew. That was what she was good at. That was safe.

But his mouth found her ear and all coherent thought vanished in a swirl of delight. His mouth ranged across her face, down her neck and across the top of her breasts. She should be touching him, kissing him, but shimmers of pleasure twirled, spinning inside her, dividing and gaining momentum until she closed her eyes to shut out everything but his touch on her. Her spine could no longer hold her up and she wrapped her legs around him and leaned back in the water, surrendering herself completely to him.

His mouth closed over her nipple and she moaned, knowing that would be the end of unhurried, that her body would buck towards his, seeking him out, not able to hold back from filling herself with him. But the touch was so surprisingly gentle, it only added to the slowly building crescendo that wove through her.

His fingers trailed down her back, then across her buttocks and across her thighs like a slow burn, until they entered her and found her heat. She moaned and tried to sit up.

'Shh, let me do this for you.' One hand supported her back while the fingers of his other hand brought a slow burn into a blazing furnace. Her breath came fast and her blood became liquid bliss. Tensing around his fingers, her body soared, colours whirled to white and she heard the sob in her voice as she cried out and shattered into a thousand pieces.

A moment later she realised tears poured down her cheeks, and she gave thanks she was in water and they couldn't be seen. What had just happened? It was like her soul had been utterly exposed, and she hated it. She'd never experienced such vulnerability in sex and she hauled herself forward, throwing herself against his chest, determined to take control. Sex was uncomplicated—it had always been uncomplicated and fun—and she wanted that reassurance back.

Her hands gripped Jack's hair and she kissed him without a trace of slowness. His thighs instantly tensed under her buttocks and she relaxed, knowing she was back on solid ground. She deepened her kiss and he met her with a hot, giving mouth as his hands tangled in her wet hair. They were two bodies on fire despite being in water and they sought each other, knowing exactly what they needed.

She gripped his shoulders and rose up slightly before lowering herself down, feeling Jack slide into her, filling her. This was how it should be. This she knew.

He moved against her, driving her upward, and she clung to him as her body took over, taking her to a place she knew, a place she sought when things got too hard, a place she'd craved for two weeks. She reached the threshold of that place and started to tumble over it when she heard her name on his lips. She stalled, suspended in time and space. Then colours rained down on her as she spun out beyond that place, pulled beyond herself and was hurled into the unknown, a part of her entwined with Jack.

CHAPTER NINE

'SHAKE a leg, girls, or we're going to be late.' Jack caught the toast and buttered it while it was hot, then packed Imogen a snack for kinder.

Sophie dashed across the sunroom, hair dripping and a towel wrapped around her, barely hiding any of her gorgeous body.

Jack grinned, remembering exactly how much of that body he'd explored this week on three separate occasions. It had taken some organisation and thinking outside the box but he'd managed to find three unique places that hadn't involved the house. Sex in the house would only remind each of them of things they'd prefer not to think about, and it had worked perfectly. If he'd thought the sex they'd had the day they met was good, it had paled into insignificance compared with what they'd shared this week. Sophie had been right—sex was cathartic; he'd never experienced such day-to-day enjoyment of life.

'Jack.' Sophie dashed back. 'Where are my clothes?'

'I brought them in off the line late last night because a storm was predicted.'

She rolled her eyes at his forward planning. 'Look

out the window. There isn't a cloud to be seen.' Her arm shot out towards the glass, only to have the towel slip.

He grinned shamelessly as she grabbed it and hoicked it back up.

'You're making a puddle, Sophie.' Imogen arrived in the room dressed in a cacophony of colours—a bright-pink T-shirt, a daisy-yellow skirt and emu-blue socks.

Sophie gave Imogen a conspiratorial smile. 'That's because Jack stole my clothes.'

Imogen nodded, her eyes dark and serious, as if she'd expected Sophie's answer. 'I didn't like the clothes Jack said to wear.'

Two sets of eyes gazed at Jack and he laughed, enjoying the way Sophie had relaxed around Im and was sharing moments like this, even if in this particular instance it was against him. Mornings were chaotic at best as they tried to get out of the door by seven-forty a.m.; he'd tried to get a system happening but it invariably fell over in some way. Right now he should be pouring coffee but his gaze wandered to the top of Sophie's towel which had slipped again to reveal a hint of creamy breast. 'I didn't steal your clothes, although that's an idea worth remembering.'

Sophie's eyes widened and the colour deepened to burnt toffee.

'Jack.' Her tone held shared memories of times when clothes had been obsolete, but it also held a warning as her head tilted slightly towards Imogen.

He snapped back into his role as the morning organiser. 'Sophie's clothes are in the laundry—and, Imogen, last night you said you wanted to wear shorts and that T-shirt, but if you want to wear your skirt that's fine. I don't care what you both wear as long as you're ready to leave in fifteen minutes.'

'Pour me some coffee, please.' Sophie clutched the towel and ran towards the laundry and Imogen climbed up onto the kitchen stool and started eating the toast.

'Jack, how many sleeps until Santa?'

'Let's see.' He passed her the chocolate advent-calendar which Im usually made a beeline for each morning. 'Today's the nineteenth. Can you find a one and a nine?'

Imogen moved her dimpled hand across the unopened cardboard doors. 'This one?'

'Yep, that's right. So, how many doors left?'

'One, two, three, four, five.'

Jack loved the way Imogen soaked up anything he chose to teach. 'This calendar ends on Christmas Eve, so we have to add one more, so that makes six sleeps until Christmas.'

Imogen popped the chocolate in her mouth and sucked it thoughtfully. 'Will Kylie be here at Christmas?'

Jack's heart ached for Im and the disappointment he was about to inflict, but there was no way he was lying to her. 'No, sweetheart, she won't be.'

Imogen kept sucking. 'What about Min?'

Jack smiled. 'Min will be here, and so will I, and so will Sophie. All of us will be at your concert.' The sudden realisation warmed him. He was looking forward to introducing Sophie to his mother because he had a feeling they'd enjoy sharing the house while he was away.

Sophie re-entered the kitchen wearing her cargo pants and a camisole top and Jack lamented the loss of the towel. The weekend was coming and he couldn't be alone with her again until Monday. Three sleeps. Three very long sleeps. He passed her a mug of coffee and a plate of fruit. 'Your breakfast order, miss.'

She smiled. 'I could get used to this sort of service, although I guess it stops when you—'

'Imogen, tell Sophie how many sleeps until the concert.'

Jack cut Sophie off, not wanting Imogen to hear about his trip, because he didn't intend to tell her until his mother was back to take his place.

Imogen wriggled excitedly on the stool. 'Five sleeps until I'm a emu.'

'Five sleeps? In that case you better try on your costume tonight to make sure it's all ready.' Taking a slug of her coffee, she looked at her watch. 'Go and clean your teeth, Imogen, so we're not late for kinder.'

'OK.'

'And bring your backpack so you can pack your snack box,' Jack called after her, pleased that for the most part—exhaustion excepted—Imogen usually did as she was told the first time she was asked, no matter if it was him or Sophie giving the instructions. The fact that Sophie had relaxed enough around Im to occasionally parent her made him smile. She'd been a lot more at ease and had even helped Imogen make a Christmas star for the kinder tree when he'd been held up at the planning meeting for the annual Barragong carols and concert.

He watched Imogen leave the room and then he leaned over the island bench towards Sophie. 'The bike I've ordered her for Christmas is coming in on this morning's courier truck. As soon as it's delivered, I'll come into the clinic.'

She shook her head, her chocolate eyes thoughtful. 'You don't have to, Jack. You do this job solo all the time; I'm only doing it for three months, and I can cope with busy days.'

'I know you can cope but it makes for a more pleasant

day if you finish at a reasonable hour and, besides, it's Friday. This way you get a swim, a proper evening meal and a relaxing evening so you can face Saturday, which sometimes is busier than a Monday.'

And you get to spend time with her.

That's the idea. With six sleeps until Christmas that meant it was only thirteen sleeps until he took off on the bike, and he planned to enjoy being with Sophie as much as he could be in the short time left.

Sophie woke with a start, her ears and eyes alert, but she sank back against her pillow when the only sound she could hear was the click-clack of the ceiling fan. She'd left the curtains open, ever hopeful of a cool breeze, and the bright-white light of the moon streamed into the room, making it as light as day. The sheet stuck to her sweaty body and she felt like she was back on the frontline, because the usually dry heat of Barragong had turned sticky and humid.

It was a surprise to be awake because she hadn't woken up in the middle of the night for the last week. She realised with a start that her wakefulness had stopped after Jack had taken her to the water hole. He'd once accused her of using sex as stress-management, and she giggled to herself, thinking she must tell him how well it was working. She could just hear him saying something along the lines of, 'for such a hypothesis to be scientifically valid, it needs a much longer testing period'—and then he'd make love to her.

She rolled over, ready to go back to sleep, but she heard the faint rumble of thunder. She got up and stared out of the window into the darkness, watching clouds scud past the moon. She thought about Jack having brought in her washing the night before because of the threat of rain. Perhaps he'd only been out by twenty-four hours. She smiled, thinking that she might owe him an apology for the crack about clear skies, but then what did he expect when he'd put her in the position of standing almost naked in front of him and Imogen?

Being naked in front of Jack was more than wonderful when they were alone, and they'd been blissfully alone three times this week. After her terrifying rush of emotions and tears at the water hole, she hadn't let Jack touch her in quite the same way. Mostly that had worked for her, and she didn't want to question why things had changed, but something had. Before Jack, sex had always been a pleasure she'd taken for herself, but now she seemed to need to wait for him to take her to release.

Another rumble of thunder drummed the air, this time louder, and all thoughts of sleep vanished. She pulled on shortie pyjamas and decided to go and watch the storm from the deck.

By the time she got to the sunroom the wind had picked up and the curtains blew out, threatening to topple the Christmas tree. She quickly dropped the wide-open window sashes and got the room under control. A flash of lightning lit up the night, followed by a loud clap of thunder, and she turned towards the French doors to see the chairs by the pool toppling over. She stepped outside into what was now a gale and hastily battened down what she could as the first few drops of rain fell coolly against her hot skin. She opened her arms up and threw her head back, but a moment later drops turned into streams and she retreated inside, wet and cold.

The sound of the rain on the old tin roof was deafening and she hugged herself, loving the noise of the rain and treasuring the moment. A thunderclap boomed overhead and she jumped in fright. The next minute she heard a scream and she ran to the hall as Imogen flung herself from her room, crying in terror.

Without thinking, Sophie picked her up and hugged her tightly, wanting to reassure her. 'Imogen, it's OK, it's just thunder and rain. You're safe.'

'Don't like it,' Imogen sobbed, clutching Sheils with one arm and Sophie with the other. 'Want Jack.'

She braced herself for the expected rush of inadequacy she normally experienced when Imogen got upset, but it didn't come. 'Shh, it's OK, Jack's just down here.' She walked down the hall to the room she hadn't entered in three weeks and opened the door.

He lay sprawled across his bed, all sleep-rumpled, dark-stubbled and obscenely handsome, virtually unconscious in a deep slumber. How he could sleep through this storm and Imogen's shrieks was beyond her.

'Jack.' She spoke softly as she sat down on the bed.

He rolled over, his heavy eyelids rising slowly, before dazed blue eyes stared up at her. 'Who what?'

Thunder cracked. Imogen wriggled out of her arms and threw herself at Jack. 'I scared.'

Jack's arms automatically closed around the little girl, like a bear protecting its cub, arms that offered security, safety and love.

An ache moved through Sophie, setting up the stirring and shifting sensation, similar to but stronger than the feeling she'd experienced when Imogen had hugged her the other day. It upended her equilibrium, spinning her every which way, setting her adrift from everything she'd ever used to anchor down her life. She swallowed a gasp. What on earth was wrong with her?

Some people call it maternal instinct.

No way. She thought of Minty—the tantrums, the

traumas and the constant feelings of hopelessness and impotence she'd experienced—and she gave herself a shake. She was so *not* maternal. She knew that, and she'd walked away from Simon because she didn't want a family. Two years later and nothing had changed. This was just crazy, middle-of-the-night, irrational nonsense.

Thunder cracked again. Imogen shrieked. Jack cuddled her close and Sophie stood up to leave. She'd delivered Imogen and she wasn't needed. Her job was done.

'Sophie.' Imogen wailed and put her arms out towards her. 'Want Sophie.'

She sat down again, her hand smoothing Imogen's curls. 'I thought you wanted to be with Jack.'

'I want you and Jack.' Imogen wriggled between them.

Jack yawned. 'Just lie down, Soph, so we can go all go back to sleep.'

Sleep? What planet was he on? The rain pummelled so loudly on the tin roof of the house that, had the noise been a rock band, they would have been hit with a hearing-protection audit. But the thought of Imogen getting more upset sent a raft of anxiety through her, so she lay down.

Imogen's warm body snuggled in; Jack's arm slung across Imogen and his hand brushed Sophie's thigh. She immediately stiffened but his fingers didn't move, didn't try to caress her, they just sat softly against her skin as if they belonged there.

Deep breaths, breathe. She forced herself to relax and she soon heard the long, slow breathing of a man descending into sleep and the gradual slowing of Imogen's breaths, until she knew both of them were fast asleep.

But sleep eluded her. She lay wide awake, listening to the rain and thinking that never in a million years could she have pictured this scenario in her life: being in bed with a man and a child. Not that it meant anything—it was just circumstances and a means to getting back to sleep.

With bodies pressed against her and being encapsulated in arms, she finally drifted off, struggling to give a name to the feeling that was the closest thing to a sense of peace she'd ever experienced.

'Jack.'

He heard his name but it sounded a long, long way away. He drowsily opened one eye and blinked against a thick red curl. Sophie's back was pressed in against his chest and her legs were wrapped around his. Bliss. He'd slept the sleep of kings.

'Jack!' This time along with the voice a small hand pushed him on the shoulder. 'Wake up, Jack.'

His mouth dried, his heart rate soared and he sat up so fast his head spun. Imogen stood by the bed, advent calendar in one hand and Sheils in the other.

'What day is today?'

Sophie sat up too, her face pale under a smattering of freckles, her eyes wide with shock and the sheet pulled up to her chin.

At least she was wearing pyjamas.

He scratched his head, vaguely remembering the storm and Sophie bringing Imogen into bed because she was scared. She wasn't scared any longer, and she wasn't even in bed, but he was, and he'd been completely wrapped around Sophie like a second skin. He swallowed a groan. 'It's number twenty today.'

'OK.' Im found the number, peeled back the cardboard and put the chocolate in her mouth. 'Can I watch TV?'

'Sure,' Jack replied weakly, relieved that television was the topic of the question and not why he'd been cuddling Sophie when there wasn't a scary storm. 'You go and get comfy on the couch and I'll be there in a minute to put on the DVD.'

'A Christmas one.'

'A Christmas one. Off you go and choose the one you want.'

Imogen ran from the room and Jack fell back on the pillow, his hands over his face.

Sophie started to laugh, the sound initially relieved before morphing into a full-on throaty chuckle. 'Oh, poor Jack. You've worked so hard to compartmentalise your life and keep everything separate, and despite all that your lover and your ward end up in your bed—no doubt along with the elephant in the room, that is what the town might think. All in all, it's your worst nightmare.'

He propped himself up on his elbow, watching her animated face, and his indignation simmered. 'I don't compartmentalise my life.'

Her face sobered. 'Sure you do. You're like Jack in *The Importance of Being Earnest*. He was Earnest in town and Jack in the country.'

She'd nailed him perfectly and he didn't like it one bit. 'That is a ridiculous analogy.'

Her brows rose arched in query. 'I'll concede you don't change your name, but you do change your personality. Think about it.' She touched his arm, her fingers gently caressing him. 'Just because your father worked out his wild streak before he settled down in Barragong, doesn't mean you have to subjugate yours and live this sedate life which isn't really you. You can still be a wonderful doctor, a worthy member of the Armitage family *and* be true to yourself, and break out now and then when the whim takes you.'

Her words punched like the jarring sound of a nail gun, but he shut them out, not wanting to think about the town, his job and following in worthy footsteps. He pulled her into his arms instead. 'I don't think you can call what we did at the water hole, the woolshed or the old mill "sedate".'

'No, it was far from sedate, thank you.' She kissed him with a light touch but then her dancing eyes clouded. 'We ran away to do it, which I don't have a problem with, but it's hardly an example of you breaking out.'

'I did it for you so you were out and away from the house and all the Christmas decorations.'

'I appreciate that, but I don't think you were being one-hundred-percent philanthropic. I worry you're letting your distorted sense of duty to the town and your family cage you.'

He stiffened. 'I don't need your worry or concern, Sophie. I'm a grown man.'

Honesty stared him down. 'All I'm saying is that you need to either leave town or find a way of living in Barragong that works for you so you can be the man you really are. I know you have this thing about the town.'

His gut clenched. 'You don't understand, Sophie. When Mary left, I was the talk of the town.'

'So you locked yourself down and took your pleasures elsewhere—I get that. But, Jack, this town loves you. You're well-respected, and I know I wasn't here, but I can imagine most of the talk would have been more to do with people being incensed with Mary rather than it being about you. Now you've trapped yourself.'

The walls of the bedroom seemed to close in on him. 'I'm not trapped. Hell, I'm leaving town in twelve days.'

'I'm not talking a physical trap, Jack.' Her brow creased. 'Perhaps in a way I am. All I know is that I've watched you with Imogen and you'd make a wonderful father, but how are you going to meet someone when you're hiding half of who you really are and letting your head jail you emotionally?'

It's me or the town, Jack. 'You're forgetting my ex-wife. She knew me, and she couldn't handle living in the fish bowl that's this town.'

She sat up and crossed her arms. 'Jack, a woman who loves you will stay. Look at your parents—your mum was happily married to your dad in this town, and from what you said they had a great partnership.'

He hated the way she'd seen down to his soul so he sat up and locked eyes with her. 'So, now you've planned out my life, let's take a look at yours, shall we? I expected you to bolt the moment Imogen woke us up. Your look was pure horror.'

'Well, she didn't look too emotionally scarred at seeing us in bed.' She leaned in close, her eyes twinkling. 'Besides, we weren't doing anything x-rated, even if you were thinking about it.'

He recognised she was flirting with him to change the subject, and he should have called her on it now he'd worked out she used sex and flirting to keep everything superficial and to protect herself. But his body overruled his brain and he joined in, holding his arms up in mock ire. 'Hey, I was asleep.'

'Your body wasn't.' She kissed him, a combination of soft, enticing pressure and hard, erotic demand, her mouth so familiar with his that she knew exactly where and how to arouse him. He remembered the sensational feeling of waking up wrapped around her. His body instantly responded.

'Jack!' Imogen's voice drifted down the hall.

He groaned and broke the kiss.

Sophie grinned. 'Tell you what, Jack—I'll help you out by going and putting on the DVD and making some tea while you make yourself decent.' She jumped out of bed and padded down the hall.

He didn't get up immediately, giving his body time to redistribute his blood from his groin. He hadn't shared his bed with a woman all night since Mary, and even then he couldn't recall feeling like this. But then this wasn't marriage with all its inherent pitfalls. What he and Sophie were sharing had absolutely nothing at all to do with real life. Sophie was gorgeous and exhilarating, but she was a fleeting visitor in his life. Despite what she'd said about how he lived, he knew exactly what he was doing, and it was the only way to be in Barragong.

The phone rang twice but stopped before his hand touched it. He sat up and pulled a T-shirt over his head, running through a mental list of Saturday chores. He'd promised to take Imogen to the Barragong gift shop so she could choose a present for his mother and Sophie, while Sophie conducted the morning clinic.

Pounding feet sounded in the hall and a moment later Sophie opened the door minus the tea tray. 'That was Max—Diana's in labour. Solid contractions, two minutes apart.'

He frowned and pulled on his shorts. 'She's four weeks early.'

Sophie twirled her hair on top of her head and jammed in a comb. 'Max says she wants you.'

'She and the baby need both of us.'

'Fine, but it's Saturday—what about Imogen?'

The solution was simple. 'She comes with us.'

Sophie set Imogen up in the nursing-home wing where she happily joined in having breakfast with the residents. 'You ask Helen if you need anything, OK?'

Imogen patted Buddy, the old golden Labrador who was the spoilt resident-dog. 'Will you come back?'

Sophie's heart hurt and she hugged her, hating that her mother had created in a lovely little girl this ever-present anxiety of being left. 'Of course I'll come back.'

Imogen's eyes stared at her, so similar in colour to her own, their gaze tainted with a hint of scepticism. 'OK.' Imogen went back to cuddling the dog.

Sophie bent down so she was the same height as the child. 'Imogen, I'm coming back. When the baby is born, I'll come and get you, I promise.'

Helen, the nurse in charge, put her hand on Sophie's shoulder. 'The residents love having visitors, and she's safe here. Now, you go and look after my best friend and help Jack deliver that longed-for baby.'

Sophie hesitated, feeling torn. Diana had Jack and a midwife, but Imogen didn't have anyone. Then again, the baby was early, and the more hands on deck the better. She bit her lip, wondering why she was vacillating. When she'd worked in a war zone she'd had to make hard decisions all the time, but one little dark-haired child had her pragmatism deserting her.

Her phone beeped with a text.

She flicked it open: *need you now!*

Her choice had been made for her. 'Soon, Imogen. I'll be back soon.'

Imogen didn't reply.

'Go now,' Helen mouthed as she put her hand out to Imogen. 'Can you help me feed Buddy?'

Sophie heard Imogen's 'Yes,' and then she turned and ran down the corridor, ducking out into the courtyard, punching in the gate's security code, hauling it open and then sprinting down the drive to the main section of the hospital.

She arrived in the labour ward panting as much as Diana.

As she opened the door she was greeted by an almighty grunting noise. 'Pushing sounds already? You're doing great, Diana.'

The nurse's contraction finished and she sank back into the pillow with a wail. 'I just want it over.'

Jack gave Diana's knee a squeeze. 'Next contraction, I want less noise and more pushing.'

Diana's green eyes flashed. 'I'm doing my best!'

'Darling, listen to Jack, he knows what he's talking about.' Max gently wiped his wife's face with a damp cloth. 'He's delivered on average about twenty babies a year for the last five years, and our baby is going to be baby one hundred.'

Jack looked stunned. 'Really?'

Max laughed. 'As CEO of the hospital, I know the stats, mate. Don't you keep count?'

'Arrgghhh.' Diana leaned forward, gripping her knees, and pushed.

Out of habit, Sophie flicked off the taps with her elbow, dried her hands and pulled on some gloves before starting her check on the paediatric set-up. A baby four weeks early could come out screaming or totally flat, and she planned to be very ready.

Jenny, the midwife, bustled through the door with the delivery-pack, saw Sophie and smiled. 'Thank goodness you're here. Rachel Pemberton's just arrived in good labour so I'll deliver her and leave you here with Jack to receive the baby.' She shook her head in bewilderment. 'I can't remember the last time two babies were born in Barragong on the same day, and so close to Christmas.'

'I caught sight of black hair that time, Diana.' Jack placed the Doppler on Diana's abdomen to check the foetal heart-rate.

Sophie heard what sounded like rapid horses' hooves and counted the beats. One hundred and five beats per minute. She bit her lip. One hundred and ten was better. She connected the tiny mask to the small air viva just in case the baby came out flat.

'Drink. Need water.' Diana leaned back, exhaustion clear on her face.

Max bent a straw and held it to his wife's mouth.

Sophie walked over to Jack, who'd stood up for a moment to stretch his back, before the next contraction had him down on the floor again. She spoke quietly. 'Anything I should know? Meconium staining of the amniotic fluid?'

He shook his head. 'So far so good. If the foetal heart drops any lower I'll use forceps, but right now we can afford to wait a bit longer. You check the foetal heart during each contraction.'

'Right. Will do.' Sophie hadn't delivered a baby since her days as a medical student and although she trusted Jack's experience and expertise, it didn't extinguish the buzz of adrenaline. Basically, they faced the unknown when this baby came out.

'Jack!' Diana pulled up against her knees, dropped her head down and pushed.

Jack dropped to his knees. 'Great work, Diana.'

'Foetal heart, one hundred.'

Diana snapped out of her contraction trance. 'That's too low.'

'Stop being a midwife, Diana, and just be a labouring woman. It's normal for the FH to drop during a contraction.' Jack sounded reassuring and stern at the same time.

Sophie squeezed Diana's hand. 'You know he's right.'

But Diana didn't answer as another contraction hit.

Five contractions later, the baby's head sat on the perineum. Jack frowned in concentration. 'OK, Diana, this time you're going to have to pant when I say, so I can guide this little one's head out and avoid stitches.'

'Need. To. Push.' A wild-eyed Diana grabbed Jack's shoulder.

'Pant, honey, pant.' Max blew up short breaths, encouraging Diana to do the same.

Sophie checked the foetal heart: ninety-five. 'Jack…'

He gave her a curt nod, having heard the slow rate and knowing this baby needed to be delivered now. He picked up the scissors. 'Diana, push hard.'

Sophie sent up a wish that Diana could deliver with this contraction and avoid the episiotomy.

With an almighty grunt, Diana pushed. Jack's fingers guided the baby's head through the perineum and out into the world.

'Well done, Diana.' Jack did a visual check for cord around the neck. 'Next contraction, we'll have a baby.'

A moment later Jack guided out the top shoulder, followed by the bottom shoulder, and then a dusky baby's body emerged.

Jack quickly passed the baby up onto Diana's stomach. 'Quick cuddle, Diana. Max, you cut the cord.'

The stunned father's hands shook as he launched his child into the world as a separate being.

'Which C is it?' Sophie asked as she hovered with the wrap.

Diana and Max checked the baby's sex together. 'Caitlyn.'

'Congratulations. But I need to take her for a minute or two.'

Max handed her the baby and Sophie quickly put her on the resus cot. Caitlyn was limp and flaccid, and her chest wasn't moving.

Don't panic. She rubbed Caitlyn's sternum with one hand while she grabbed the mask with the other. Using the mask on the tiny face, she puffed in air.

She could hear Jack's voice giving instructions as he delivered the placenta but it was just background noise as every part of her focused on the baby. *Come on, baby girl.* She continued to puff in air and slowly the dusky colour of Caitlyn's skin started to pink up and her chest started to rise and fall on her own. She checked the baby's heart rate which had risen to one hundred and ten.

'Is everything all right?' Diana's anxious voice called across the room.

Right on cue, Caitlyn cried, loudly and lustily.

Sophie blew out a long breath. 'Everything's fine. Apgars at one minute are eight.'

'Thank God.' Max kissed his wife with gratitude and relief. 'Thank you.'

Jack walked over to the cot and beamed. He put his finger against Caitlyn's palm and the baby immediately gripped it. 'Welcome to the world, baby girl.' He wrapped her up in a bunny rug and picked her up.

Sophie's knees shook as she watched Jack cradling the tiny baby in his strong arms, and holding her close against his broad chest. She knew those arms could be a wonderful haven, a retreat from the world, a place of safety and security. Jack was a natural father, and any baby would be lucky to be in those arms.

What about a baby of yours?

The thought hit her with all the winding power of a punch to the solar plexus. This was crazy thinking. She didn't want a child. Sure, she'd coped with Imogen these last two weeks, but only just. She constantly held her breath expecting the screams and the tantrums that Minty had specialised in, and feared she'd crack again like she'd done with the train.

No, this stray thought was just a reaction to the relief of a safe delivery. The come-down from the adrenaline-fuelled high which had sent her thoughts charging toward things she knew were not for her.

Jack's violet eyes, often so piercing and insightful, glowed with the same softness she saw in his gaze when he watched Imogen. Then he raised them to her and smiled.

A smile part-bad-boy, part-Armitage, part-doctor and all Jack.

The world tilted and spun out from under her in a seismic shift. She gripped the side of the resus cot to stay standing. Dear God, she loved him.

How could you have let this happen?

Her breath came jerkily as she realised she'd been fooling herself. For the past couple of weeks she'd told herself she was only attracted to the wild side of Jack and that what they shared was all about sex. She'd rationalised that she respected the doctor that was Jack, and she begrudgingly put up with the organised, overly responsible Jack who drove her nuts. But her rationalisation had all been flim-flam nonsense. She loved all of him: the wild, fun-loving, nurturing, caring man. A man who once he'd taken his holiday would come back to Barragong and stay. A man who deserved a family.

'Soph, you OK? You're looking a bit pale.' Jack had passed Caitlyn to her parents and all his astute and caring attention was now completely fixed on her.

Think. Her heart beat so fast it fluttered, and she gave herself a shake, trying to firm up her collapsed world so that Jack didn't twig that anything was amiss. 'I'm fine. Caitlyn had me worried for a moment, and I haven't had breakfast, so that combination made me just a bit wobbly. It's nothing that a shot of coffee and the sugar high of a croissant and jam won't fix. I'll grab something when I collect Imogen. I promised her that the moment the baby was born I'd go and get her.'

Surprise flitted across his face. 'OK. Grab me something too, please, and I'll clean up here.'

She nodded and brushed past him, stopping by the ecstatic parents who'd moved up onto the bed and were gazing in wonder at their new daughter. 'Is it OK if Imogen comes in and has a quick cuddle?'

Diana, now full of the energy of post-labour endorphins, beamed. 'We'd love it. Our family have to drive up from Adelaide so they won't be here until this afternoon. Im can be our first visitor.'

Relief poured through her. 'Thanks, back soon.' Without looking back at Jack, Sophie escaped into the corridor.

CHAPTER TEN

JACK cuddled Caitlyn while Diana had a shower and Max telephoned his parents. 'You're my baby one hundred. How did that happen?' He couldn't believe he'd helped to bring that many children into the world. Into Barragong.

We do good work, Jack, be proud of it.

Max snapped his phone shut and strode over, his wide smile filled with gratitude. 'Thanks, mate. It's pretty special that our daughter can be born in the town she's going to call home, and that only happened because of you. Without you, Di would have to have gone to Adelaide.'

'It's my pleasure.' The words he spoke to patients so often as an automatic response now resonated with feeling. 'I'm glad I was here.' And he was. The ever-present slightly disgruntled feeling that had dogged him for five years had vanished, leaving him feeling buoyant and happy. Elation flowed through him but he couldn't put his finger on why. Nothing in Barragong had changed.

Sophie's the reason.

Diana came out of the bathroom, her face wreathed in a smile.

'Maybe that's why Caitie here came early. She was

taking her chance, wanting you to deliver her, knowing you'd be on the road on her due date.'

A knock sounded at the door and then Sophie ushered Imogen into the room and directed her to a chair. 'You sit there and then you can cuddle the baby for a minute. I'll hold Sheils for you.'

Imogen scrambled onto the chair, and Sophie bobbed down next to her so she could help support the baby.

'I ready, Jack.' With shining eyes, Imogen held out her little arms.

Jack grinned and carefully placed the baby across her lap. Sophie ran her arm along the baby's length as an extra protection.

Imogen stared at the baby and then looked up at Diana. 'Your baby can be in the 'tivity play.'

Diana smiled. 'Do you think Caitlyn would like to lie in the manger?'

Imogen nodded seriously. 'And the wombats will give her presents.'

'That's a great idea, Im.' Jack watched the little girl holding the baby, her dark head bent over next to Sophie's titian curls.

Sophie helped Imogen support Caitlyn's head and they laughed together as the baby's tiny hand escaped from the bunny rug and gripped one of Sophie's curls. Together, they glanced up at Jack, two pairs of smiling chocolate eyes.

He laughed and smiled back at his girls.

His girls.

Sheer joy exploded inside him, rocking him to his core. His girls. He'd been so busy planning his trip, aching to get out of town, that he'd been totally blind to the two best things that had ever happened to him.

Sophie had stormed into his life, turned it upside

down, challenged every one of his misguided beliefs, and he loved her.

I love her.

He held his breath, waiting for the terror to strike, and for the fear that came with being in a relationship and sharing his life with her. But the only thing exploding inside him was happiness and excited anticipation at spending the rest of his life with her. A picture formed in his mind of Imogen holding a baby with red curly hair.

Being a father is a very special thing.

The iron bars that had surrounded him for five years vaporised. He knew without a doubt he belonged in this town and that Imogen belonged with him. The thought of her going to another family was inconceivable and, paperwork and a rubber stamp aside, he knew he'd just become a father.

They were a family. Sophie and Imogen were his family. The thought settled over him in a comforting cloak and for the first time he truly felt he'd really come home to Barragong.

Sophie doesn't want children.

The thought dragged through him like barbed wire, snagging on skin. He glanced at Sophie who'd just lifted the baby out of Imogen's arms and was carrying her back to her mother. She held the baby in the crook of her arm, her gaze centred on Caitlyn. Jack had never seen such a look of yearning on Sophie's face.

He knew right then, without a shadow of a doubt, that she wanted a child. She wanted exactly what he wanted.

She laid the baby in Diana's arms and as she straightened up he caught her gaze. Emotions swirled, mixing and separating, but in the whirlpool he saw love.

The bubble of happiness inside him expanded even further. The future rolled out in front of him in such brilliant 3D-clarity that his hand reached out to grab it.

Sophie leaned over the deck, watched the blazing sunset, heard the song of the cicadas and tried to let her spinning mind still. It had been a hell of a weekend and she hadn't seen anything of Jack or Imogen since an hour after Caitlyn's birth. Saturday afternoon there'd been an accident involving a road train and a caravan, and she'd worked with the flying doctors to evacuate five people to Adelaide. She'd only just fallen asleep when her phone had woken her and she'd dashed back to the hospital to treat two children with asthma attacks, as well as admitting an elderly patient with chest pain.

Daylight hadn't brought any relief from the frantic pace, and the tiny emergency department had been flat out with a rush of pre-Christmas-excitement injuries: a child had swallowed a plastic whistle from a bon-bon; a father had badly burned his arm on a barbecue; another had crushed his finger assembling a trampoline. She'd finally arrived home an hour ago just in time to say goodnight to Imogen.

In between cases she'd tried to process her emotions. The fact that she'd fallen in love with Jack had left her shocked, rudderless and drifting, but she'd dug deep and decided that although her love for Jack was appallingly inconvenient for her nothing between them had to change. Jack need never know she loved him, and no way was she going to tell him. The fact he didn't love her was the only salvageable thing in this whole mess. At least she wouldn't hurt him like she'd hurt Simon.

They could walk away from each other just as they'd planned.

She had ten days left with Jack. Ten days to soak him up and keep her traitorous emotions well under wraps. When he left for his trip, she'd clear out the hospital flat and move in there for the last two months of her contract, leaving the house for Jack's mother and Imogen to enjoy. By the time Jack returned to town—if he returned to town—she'd be long gone, starting work on another contract. Vanuatu appealed and she'd already emailed the agency.

The sun dipped behind the purple ranges but nothing dented the heat. Her father had emailed her, telling her of icy weather, frozen pipes and the village locked in by snow. The village children were very excited that this year would be a white Christmas, and he was equally thrilled that Minty and Amelia had arrived home to help celebrate. The unspoken message was, 'it's been too long; wish you were here'.

Sorry, Dad. Maybe next year.

The thought totally surprised her, because a month ago she would never have even contemplated the idea of going home for Christmas—but then again she'd never contemplated living in a house where the run up to Christmas was a tradition in itself. She'd survived the tree, the baking, the crafts and the stories Imogen insisted she read. Who knew Australia had their own version of *The Twelve Days of Christmas* and that white kangaroos pulled the sleigh?

You've more than survived it.

She hugged herself tightly and blew out a long breath. She'd not only fallen in love with Jack, she'd rediscovered the joy of Christmas in this house on the other side of the world. When Jack left on his trip, she'd thank him for that.

She heard the click of the French doors, felt Jack's arms snake around her waist and then felt his mouth nuzzle her neck. Lust tangled up with cosy warmth, the sensation she now recognised as love. She tried to ignore it by tapping into lust but her brain did a double take. *He never touches you in the house if Imogen's home too.*

She shut out common sense; she closed her eyes and leaned back into him, absorbing his scent and touch, soaking it in and banking it for the long, lonely nights ahead of her.

He kissed her hair. 'Im's fast asleep.'

She yawned. 'I don't think I'm too far away from that state.'

'Is that so?' His lips and tongue found the sensitive spot behind her ear.

She gasped as her body fired shimmering pleasure into every cell, rolling fatigue away fast. She turned in his arms and met his gaze that was filled with the familiar longing for her, but she glimpsed something unfamiliar and undefined hovering behind it.

'Still tired?' He tucked a curl behind her ear. 'I could tuck you up in bed.'

She traced his jaw with her forefinger. 'That's a very generous offer.'

'I'm a very generous guy.'

She laughed, loving the way he made her feel. 'You do realise that tucking me in would involve us being in a bedroom together in this house?'

'I don't have a problem with that.'

He smiled down at her, his smile devoid of the flirting lust she was so used to seeing. Instead, care and devotion had taken its place and her heart cramped as a hint of panic jetted through her.

She pushed back slightly, trying to give herself space to think. 'Yes, you do. You have an inflexible rule about sex in this house because of Imogen and the town.'

He arm tugged her back against him. 'I *did* have a rule.'

Quicksand warning. Soft-cliff edge. Avalanche area. 'What's changed?'

'Everything.' He gazed at her, his heart in his eyes. 'I love you, Sophie, and I want to make love to you in our house.'

Silver spots danced in front of her eyes and all her blood drained to her feet. This couldn't be happening. It wasn't happening; she wouldn't let it. She struggled to hold on to rational thought. 'You don't love me, Jack. You just love the sex. We both do, and why not? It's great sex—but it ends next week when you take your trip.'

He shook his head. 'I'm not going.'

Her chest wouldn't move and she struggled to get her breath. 'What are you talking about? Of course you're going. It's your dream, what you've wanted for years.'

He shook his head. 'It *was* my dream, but it's not now. Yesterday everything changed. I love you, Sophie, and I want to marry you.'

Her knees sagged but somehow she launched herself out of his arms and gripped the deck-railing, unable to keep up with the bombshells he was dropping faster than a B52.

'You don't want to marry me. You don't to marry anyone again; you told me that.'

His eyes crinkled around the edges. 'That was before you stormed into my life, changed all the rules and showed me how things could be so very different.' A quiet calm encircled him. 'The trip isn't important any more, Soph, but we are.'

No, we're not. A violent tremble started at her toes and rocked through her, shaking her entire body. She wrapped her arms around herself, trying to control it. 'Jack, you have to take this trip. You have to taste the freedom you've wanted so badly for so long.'

He came to stand next her, his expression filled with love. 'These last couple of weeks we've been together have been the best thing that has ever happened to me. Out of a sequence of unfortunate events has risen a family.' He reached out and rested his hand on her shoulder. 'Kylie doesn't want Imogen and I've decided to be her permanent foster-father. I love her, I love you. We're a family.'

A family. Her stomach rolled and bile scalded her throat. *Oh God, no. I'm going to hurt him so much.* 'You want to marry me and adopt Imogen?'

His eyes shone with pleasure. 'I do.' His hand covered hers on the rail. 'I saw how you looked at Caitlyn yesterday, and I'm hoping we can give Im a baby brother or sister or two. Together we can do this, and we'll make great parents.'

Her breathing shot to short, shallow breaths and the dizziness increased. She dug deeper than she'd ever done in her life and somehow managed to gulp air down into her tight lungs and stop herself from passing out. She met his gaze, hating herself for not being able to give him what he wanted, what he deserved.

'I didn't mean for you to fall in love with me, Jack. You're a good man, but I'd make you miserable, because I don't want what you want. I haven't seen the three of us as a family. Hell, I spend every day on egg shells, expecting to do the wrong thing with Imogen. I don't want a family or to live in one place forever. This house, your family, that sort of history—it's not me.'

'It could be.'

His naïve belief pulled at her so strongly she almost walked into his arms. 'Jack, this is totally crazy.'

He grinned. 'No, it's totally right. We belong together.'

I'll hurt you, and you deserve so much better than that. 'No, we don't. You need to take your trip and I need to work for you and then leave town. That's the plan.' She heard her voice rising. 'You're the man who plans everything, so why the hell aren't you sticking to this one?'

He stroked her cheek. 'Because you've taught me that my life can be so much more than what it's been, and the plan no longer fits either of us.'

His calmness terrified her, ramping up her agitation. 'My plan of leaving still fits perfectly.'

He picked up her hands, his thumbs making gentle circles across the tops of her knuckles. 'I watched you holding Caitlyn yesterday and the look on your face mirrored mine. I think that mothering Imogen has put the ghosts of your past to bed and now your life plan of not having children needs revising. It's time to stop running.'

She longed for the scream of rockets and all the other dangers of a war zone because it was so much safer than this. She tugged her hands out from under his as an ache spread through her. 'I haven't mothered Imogen.'

His eyebrows rose. 'You've taken her to and from kinder, reminded her to clean her teeth and made her an emu costume.'

'That's childcare, not mothering. It comes under the "responsible adult" banner you wave all the time.'

Incredulity rolled across his handsome face. 'It's been so much more than that. You've cuddled up with her in bed, read her stories and splashed and laughed with her in the pool. I've watched you unwind around her, seen you enjoy her—and the other night when she refused to eat dinner you were the one that kept your cool, not me.' His hand rested gently on her shoulder. 'Let the past go, Soph, and trust yourself that you can do this. You're not a teenager any more, you're a mature woman, and it's time you accepted you're a good mother.'

His words rained down on her, terrifying her. She didn't dare believe him, didn't dare consider staying, because if he was wrong—and she was sure he was—she'd hurt both Imogen and Jack even more than if she left now. 'I don't want this, Jack. I want my freedom.'

'Freedom?' He snorted. 'You don't have freedom, Sophie, you're too busy running to be free. What are you going to do—spend your life going from war zone to war zone until you fall in a heap? You deserve better than that. You aren't living your life, you're running from it, and it's time to stop. This so-called freedom you believe in is just fear.'

Everything inside her stilled. Like the knife that had pared into her palm and sliced down to her tendon, he'd just sliced through every protective layer she'd ever wrapped around herself and exposed the truth. The truth that held all her worst fears. Fear that she would hurt who she loved—hurt an innocent child. Fear she couldn't be the woman Jack wanted as the mother of his children.

Pain lacerated her and she knew she had to do the hardest thing she'd ever done in her life—make him not want her to stay at all.

'I'm not one of your projects, Jack, and I don't need saving.'

Jack heard a brittle hardness in Sophie's voice he'd never encountered. It ate at the edges of his belief that he was right, and that with some encouragement she would realise that being with him and Imogen was what she wanted most in the world. 'I think you need Im and I in your life.'

She tossed her head, her eyes flashing. 'You think wrong. This is your problem, Jack. It's your over-developed sense of duty getting in the way of what you really want. Yes, Imogen needs a family, but it's not your job to marry me and provide it. Think about it, Jack—if you marry me and adopt Imogen, it's a repeat scenario of what made you so unhappy when your father died. You came back here earlier than you wanted to and married Mary because you thought the doctor in town should be settled. It's made you resentful, and you need to take your trip, because if you don't you'll end up resenting Imogen.'

'You're right about my marriage but you're way off the mark with Imogen.' A slow, burning anger curled through his belly like a snake as incredulity rocked him. She didn't get it; she had no clue. 'I can't believe you're suggesting I leave Imogen for three months.'

Her arms folded tightly across her chest. 'I'm trying to get you to see sense.'

He threw his arm out towards the house. 'There's a little girl in there who's been abandoned by her mother and she needs all the stability I can give her.'

For less than a second her gaze wavered and then she tilted her chin. 'And your mother will provide that while you're away.'

He stared at her, wondering if he really knew her

at all—if yesterday he'd misread the love and care in her eyes for him and Imogen. 'Oh, right—I take a self-ish holiday and destroy the fledgling trust I've started to build up with her, and instead instil such a level of anxiety that she spends the next five years waiting for me to leave. Won't that make adolescence fun?'

She didn't say a word, and his conviction that she loved him and Imogen was snuffed out like a flame starved of oxygen. Memories of Mary hovered—arms crossed and ultimatums issued.

A woman who loves you will stay.

Sophie had spoken those words to him yesterday morning.

Nothing about her body language hinted at her stay-ing, and the reality of the situation fell irreparably into place. 'You're going to turn your back on Imogen and I and leave, aren't you?'

She bit her lip, her face pale under her freckles. 'It's better that I go now. Better for you and Imogen.'

His heart ripped in half and he gripped the railing so hard he thought he'd crush it. 'How do you figure that?'

'You'll hate me less for it now than later.'

Her words crushed him. 'That's the only thing you've said that makes any sense.' Then, unable to stop it, he felt his lip curl, he gave into anger and let hurt have full rein. 'But I was forgetting you're an expert at this, having already left Simon for the same reason.'

She recoiled as if he'd slapped her across the cheek.

He thought he heard her mumble, 'I didn't love him,' but he realised that was just his own desperate imagination.

When she finally spoke, her words were loud and clear and her face distant and determined. 'I've never pretended to you that I wanted a family or a relationship.'

'That's because you're too busy pretending you don't.'

'I'm sorry, Jack.' It came out as a plea.

But he didn't want to stay and listen to nonsensical platitudes, and no way in hell was he offering her absolution. 'Move your stuff into the Barragong Motel and book yourself on the Boxing Day bus. Your last day of duty is Christmas Day.'

She didn't even flinch at the date he'd deliberately chosen to hurt her with as he tried to offset his own pain which ran so deep.

'What will you tell Imogen—?'

Her voice cracked on the little girl's name but he had no sympathy for her. She'd made her choice abundantly clear. He glared at her, so angry and so bereft that he wanted to sob, but with Herculean effort he held it together. 'What I tell her is none of your concern. Your leaving forfeits that right.'

He heard her shocked gasp but he didn't wait for a reply. Wrenching open the door, he strode to Imogen's room. Standing quietly in the doorway he watched his daughter sleep, seeking refuge in the one constant that made sense in his life when all his hopes and dreams had turned to ash.

'Diana's champing at the bit to be discharged.' Jenny, the straight-talking midwife, greeted Sophie as she arrived on to the ward. 'I rang Jack thinking he might come in and do it this morning, because I know you've been flat out, but he says he's not working and you're it. You look like hell, by the way.'

Sophie tried to smile and act like everything was

as normal as it had been last week, even though absolutely nothing came close to resembling normal. 'It's Christmas Eve; Jack's minding Imogen and he's probably busy preparing for tonight's carol service.'

Jenny frowned. 'That accounts for today, but what about the last forty-eight hours? You two have shared the clinic and hospital patients for the last three weeks and juggled Imogen between you, so why change now?'

Because I hurt him; because he hates me. 'Jack's technically on holidays, and I'm the one supposed to be working.' Sophie grabbed Diana's chart out of the midwife's hands. 'I better go and see her before she checks herself out.'

She hurried down the corridor, desperate to escape Jenny's questions. She knew she looked like death warmed up but there wasn't much she could do about that, seeing as she hadn't slept in three nights. The motel wasn't anything stunning, but even if she'd been in a five-star international hotel she still wouldn't have been able to sleep.

Why was doing the right thing so hard? She loved Jack but she had to leave him, because she'd only let him down when she made a hash of motherhood, and then it would all end in acrimony. She would have done anything to leave town two days ago but she had a contract to honour, even though Jack was cutting it off early. He'd played hardball, insisting she stay until Boxing Day, but she knew he'd done that for Imogen because he didn't want to be on call until his mother was home.

Will you come back? She tried to stop the agitated feeling that thudded through her whenever she thought of Imogen. For the umpteenth time she told herself that she was the adult and by leaving now she was protecting the child. Besides, it had only been three short weeks, and it was unlikely that Imogen would have really become attached to her. Jack was her main carer and when anything went wrong it was Jack who Imogen wanted.

But her heart kept disagreeing with her head, sending nausea swilling through her gut. *You've let her down badly.* She entered Diana's room and her feet stopped as if glued to the floor. Baby Caitlyn was snuggled at her mother's breast, gulping in milk, and Diana gazed down at her daughter, cocooning her in love.

A pain lanced Sophie so sharply, she almost doubled over. *You could have had this.*

I'd ruin it.

'How are mother and daughter doing?'

Diana glanced up with a smile, which wavered before creasing into a slight frown. 'Better than you, by the looks of it. Has A&E gone troppo?'

'Sorry I didn't make it before lunch.' Sophie stroked the baby's head. 'How's she been feeding?'

'She's doing so well for a thirty-six weeker that I'm thinking perhaps my dates were wrong.'

'She's certainly more awake than the average prem baby, and she's gained weight, which is what we like to see. My only concern is her slight jaundice, so keep an eye on that, and if she does get sleepy bring her in.'

Diana nodded her understanding. 'I'll let the early-morning sunshine come in for some natural phototherapy.'

'Good idea.' Sophie smiled. 'Do you have any questions before I officially discharge you?'

Diana eased the now-sleeping Caitlyn off the breast. 'Can you hold her for a minute?'

Sophie hesitated. She'd prefer not to have anything to do with children at the moment.

'You won't break her.' Diana held her daughter out towards her, her gaze disconcertingly direct.

Sophie's arms started to throb with an ache very familiar to most women, an ache dating back to the dawn of time. She slid them around the swaddled baby and breathed in the fresh, baby scent—but instead of the sweet, milky aroma she could suddenly smell apples and freshly washed hair so strongly it was as if both were in the room with her. The memory of the scent of Imogen's shampoo, the sight of tangled, wet curls, and the touch of a warm, slippery body as she threw herself into the fluffy towel that Sophie always held up, thundered through her. Tears pricked her eyes and her heart bled. *I did the right thing, though, didn't I?*

Diana adjusted her feeding bra and buttoned up her blouse. 'I go through almost as many clothes as Caitie does.'

Sophie tried to smile but her mouth refused to curve upwards. 'How are you finding it?'

'It?' Diana looked perplexed.

'Motherhood.'

'It's only day five, but we're learning together. I think that's what being a mother is all about, or at least that's what my mother tells me. Often you're only one step ahead of the kid, and sometimes you're a step behind.'

Sophie knew exactly what she meant. She'd always felt a giant step behind with Minty, and a few steps with Imogen, although just lately she'd had moments of being ahead. 'Doesn't that scare you? I mean, what if you make a mistake?'

The new mother pondered the question. 'I don't think I'm scared. A bit nervous, perhaps.' She gave a wry laugh. 'I know I'll probably make a heap of mistakes, because that goes with the territory, but I'll be doing my absolute best and that's all I can do.' She smiled serenely. 'I've got Max to balance off against, so you've got to hope one of us will have our act together if the other one is floundering.'

We'll make great parents. She pushed away Jack's beguiling voice. She knew the truth about herself even if he refused to recognise it.

Diana eyes studied Sophie's face. 'What's going on, Sophie? Max says Jack looks as drawn as you do.'

She handed Caitlyn back. 'It's the heat.'

'It's way more than the heat.' Diana's hand touched her arm. 'I don't understand. I've seen the way the two of you have been looking at each other since you arrived. Everyone in town's talking about how good you are together, and how great you both are with Imogen.'

'Jack's the one who's great with Imogen. Unlike me, he's a natural with children.' Sophie stood up and pulled out her stethoscope. 'Let's examine this little one so you can take her home.'

Diana unwrapped the baby from the bunny rug. 'Jack does have an unnatural amount of patience. We've all tried to hate him for it, especially when we get annoyed and snap when some kid has pushed us to the end of our rope. But he's no saint, Sophie, and he does crack sometimes.'

You were the one that kept your cool, not me. She thought back to the dinner when Imogen had refused to eat her vegetables. They'd all been hot and tired, and she'd had to fight so hard against yelling and falling apart. But it was Jack who'd got cross. She'd been the one to compromise with Imogen, trading off carrots and capsicum against the refused broccoli.

But so many other times she'd floundered, not really knowing if she was doing the right thing or not—mostly listening to her gut and always second guessing her decisions. Was that what being a mother was all about—instinct, not science?

She rolled her shoulders back. She was a doctor who dealt with facts; she might not know how to be a mother but she knew exactly how to be a doctor. Shoving the stethoscope into her ears, she listened to Caitlyn's heart and checked her reflexes, her hips and spine before putting the nappy back on.

Diana gave her a speculative look. 'You know, you're pretty good yourself with Imogen, considering you had the harder job.'

Sophie's hand stalled on the nappy pin. 'What do you mean?'

'Jack's known Imogen on and off for five years, but you've only been in her life for three weeks. He has the history and the emotional attachment, and Im trusts him. But to Im you were just another stranger in the parade of many who've moved through her life. You've done an awesome job, getting her to trust you so quickly. I think you just need to start trusting yourself.'

I hate you, Sophie.

I want Sophie.

She gave the nappy pin a hard push through the layers of material. 'Life's just not that simple, Diana.'

'It doesn't have to be complicated, either.' Diana leaned over, picked up a hand-made card and passed it to Sophie. On the cover was a child's drawing of a couple with a baby. 'Im drew this for Max, Caitlyn and I. Open it.'

Sophie turned over the cover and inside was a picture of three stick figures—a little girl with curly black hair holding hands with a tall man with black hair and a woman whose head was twice as wide with huge, red curls. All wore huge smiles.

We're a family. Im had drawn the three of them as a family. The family Imogen wanted. The family Jack wanted.

It's time you accepted you're a good mother.

You're not a teenager any more, you're a mature woman. Trust yourself that you can do this.

Her heart both cried and sang at the same time and a tear rolled down her cheek. *A family.* She wanted this.

Will you come back?

Of course I'll come back.

Her breath stalled as maternal pain tore through so hard and fast it almost ripped her in half. What had she done? She'd been given the gift of unconditional love from a wonderful man and a gutsy little girl, and she'd run from their love because she didn't trust herself.

She'd broken Imogen's trust. She'd made Jack hate her.

And all for what? Jack had been right; he'd seen straight through her. She'd been letting fear rule her life and now she'd lost everything she'd ever needed. A sob caught in her throat as she recalled Jack's harsh and unforgiving expression when he'd ordered her out of the house.

How did she even start to make amends and get back her family she'd so badly rejected?

CHAPTER ELEVEN

SOPHIE stumbled to her feet, dizzy with the need to see Jack and Imogen and to try to make everything right. 'Caitlyn's fine to make her debut in the kinder nativity-play in a few hours.'

'Sophie, sit down, you're ashen.'

She ignored the nurse's command and ran from the room, dumping her white coat at the desk, grabbing her phone and pager and sprinting to the car park. She turned on the ignition and floored the accelerator, sending gravel flying as she sped down the road. Five minutes later she got stuck behind a slow sheep-transport truck, and the stream of cars heading into town for the evening's Christmas Eve festivities prevented her from overtaking. The usual fifteen-minute trip turned into twenty-five, and she almost wept.

Turning at the *Santa, please stop here* sign, she bounced down the track and roared in over the cattle grid. Jack's vehicle was in the drive parked alongside a Mercedes Kompressor. Her heart quivered as panic fluttered in her chest. All she'd been able to think about since leaving the hospital was getting to the Armitage house and finding Jack. Talking to Jack.

She hadn't anticipated visitors. Her head spun and her chest heaved, her breath coming way too fast. She pushed back from the steering wheel and blew out a long, slow breath, trying to get herself under control. This was her one shot at happiness and she had to get it right.

She started to walk up the front steps, planning on ringing the bell, when she heard voices—male and female—shouting out Imogen's name.

Jack strode around the veranda and stopped short. His thick hair, usually so neat, was spiked up as if his hands had ploughed through it and his handsome face was haggard. 'What the hell are you doing here?'

His words stabbed bluntly through her heart. 'I need to talk to you, I—'

'I don't want to talk to you.' He marched past her, making a funnel with his hands, and called out, 'Im?'

An older woman's voice called out in the distance, 'Imogen, come back, sweetheart. Immy.'

A sliver of dread crawled across Sophie's skin. 'Jack, where's Imogen?'

He turned, his eyes sparking white like flint, but that didn't disguise the desperation and fear. 'Do you really care?'

The bullet hit, ripping through her, but before she could reply a woman similar in age to Jack ran around the front of the house. 'She's not in the chook shed, the tree house, the sandpit, swing set or the pool.'

An older woman who Sophie recognised instantly as Jack's mother stepped out of the front door onto the veranda. 'I've been through the cottage garden twice and she's not there.'

'And I've checked under the house, the garage and the shed.' Jack ran his hand across the back of his neck. 'Ring the police, Mum, and get a search party happening. Jules, you double back and check out the garden again, and I'll take the quad bike down the back track in case she wandered down there.'

'Down there' was the gorge, a place full of dangers for an adult, let alone a five-year-old. Panic morphed into full-blown fear. Sophie grabbed Jack's arm, pulling hard to stop him from walking down the steps. 'How long has she been gone?'

'An hour.'

Her heart cramped. That was a long time for a child to be lost in this heat, in the vast expanse of outback that surrounded them. She thought back over the last three weeks, all the hours and days she'd spent with Imogen. If anything, she tended to be clingy because of her mother's abandonment and always wanted to stay close for cuddles and stories. Her sudden disappearance didn't make any sense. 'But why would she wander off? She's never done that before.'

Jack's hand grasped hers and threw it off his arm. 'This is *your* fault, Sophie.'

His anger and pain blasted through her so hard she swayed and needed to grab hold of a veranda post to keep her upright.

'Jack.' Min shook her head as if to say, 'don't; concentrate on Imogen'.

This is your *fault.* Sophie struggled not to let fear and guilt envelop her and steal away all her control. Had Imogen been so distraught by her leaving that she'd run away? A wail rose in her chest but somehow she forced it back down. There'd be a lifetime for recriminations, but right now she had to find her little girl.

'Where did you see her last?' Sophie heard the plea in her voice as she glanced around at everyone.

'We've got this covered, Sophie. You can leave.' Jack held his arm out towards the steps, dismissing her.

Min sighed and turned to Sophie. 'It was just as Juliet arrived. Immy was so excited about the concert and was begging us to let her wear her costume. We'd given in and said she could wear it but that she had to play quietly with the Christmas train, and that's what she was happily doing. We walked down the hall to greet Juliet, and when we walked back she was gone.'

Where could she be? The heat haze from the red earth beyond the garden shimmered, mocking her, saying that the desert could so easily swallow up a child and never return her. *You've lost her.*

No, I have not! She closed her ears to the argument in her head, to the fears that plagued her, just like she'd used to block out the noise of the falling bombs. She sought the place where she could really think.

I like to play here.

Sophie instantly remembered the time Imogen had vanished on her when she'd been playing quietly and an idea rushed in. 'Have you checked inside the house?'

'God, Sophie, do you think we're stupid? Of course we've checked the house.' Jack stormed towards the steps.

'I think I might know where she is.' Without stopping to explain, she pulled the wire door open and ran down the hall, calling over her shoulder, 'Mrs Armitage, is it OK if I go into your room?'

'Of course it is.'

Sophie's heart thundered against her ribs. *Imogen, darling, be here—please be here.* She wrenched open the wardrobe door and reached in, pulling on the light. She started to cry, great, racking sobs that came from so deep they shuddered all the way through her as she tossed out shoe boxes and hat boxes and Christmas presents. She fell to her knees and crawled in.

Tears blurred her vision, but she could make out a familiar shape. Imogen lay fast asleep in the far corner of the wardrobe, her head on a cushion and her arms wrapped around Sheils. Somehow, between sobs, Sophie found her voice and yelled out, 'I've found her.'

She hauled the child into her arms, buried her face in her apple-scented hair and let her tears fall.

'Jack, Sophie's found her.'

She heard Min's voice calling out faintly in the distance.

Imogen slowly opened her eyes, blinked and then smiled. 'I hided, but they didn't find me.'

Sophie smiled and sniffed. 'They didn't know about our special place, did they?' She stroked Imogen's hair. 'But we need to tell everyone about it because they thought you were lost.'

The little girl shook her head with all the logic of a child. 'I wasn't lost, I was here. Why are you crying?'

Sophie wiped her face with the back of her hand. 'Because I've missed you.'

Imogen snuggled in. 'Jack says doctors have to work at the hospital.'

More tears spilled out, rolling down already damp cheeks. Jack might hate her, but he hadn't bad-mouthed her to Imogen. A flicker of hope flared for a moment before dying away. Did that mean anything more than the fact that Jack was a good and decent man? Probably not. God, her life was the biggest mess. 'Come on, honey, let's go and show everyone you're OK.'

Footsteps pounded on the floorboards as Sophie nudged Imogen out of the wardrobe. She didn't follow. She heard Jack's voice, gruff with emotion, Min's and Juliet's sweeter tones telling her how worried they'd been, and that if she wanted to play hide and seek she must tell them before hiding.

The voices faded away along with the footsteps and Sophie sat with her head on her knees, psyching herself to leave the relative safety of the hiding space before she launched herself once more into her self-created, personal hell. Could she get Jack to speak with her? He'd made it pretty clear he didn't want to have anything to do with her.

When the room had been silent for a couple of minutes, she crawled backwards out of the wardrobe, stood up, turned around and gasped.

Jack sat on his mother's bed, dishevelled, gorgeous and grim. Her heart rolled over. Nothing resembling forgiveness hovered on his cheeks, only chilled resentment.

His violet eyes bored into her. 'How did you know she was in there?'

She tilted her chin and met his gaze, knowing only the truth could save her. Save them. 'Maternal instinct.'

His body jerked as if he'd been shocked by a jolt of electricity. 'Three days ago you insisted you didn't have any of that.'

'I know. I was wrong.'

'Wrong?' His brows rose with scepticism.

She nodded, biting her lip hard. 'I've been wrong about everything.'

'You're right about that.' But his frosty expression had thawed slightly and the harsh corner of his mouth had softened.

A strangled sound escaped her lips and she fell to her knees, seeking forgiveness. The tension in his body slammed hard against her, screaming emotional ruthlessness and judgement, but she centred herself and kept on going. 'I've made a complete hash of everything,

Jack. I couldn't see the future like you could and I was so scared I'd ruin it that I ran from it, just like you accused me of doing.'

He held himself stiffly, his hands fisted by his side. 'What brought you back?'

'You. Imogen.'

His throat convulsed, but still he didn't touch her. 'How do I know you're not going to run again at the first hard moment?'

She stared up into his violet eyes, knowing she'd violated his trust in her so badly that it was only by baring her soul that she could attempt to repair the damage. 'Because you and Imogen are the only things in my life that make sense. I love her and I love you, Jack. You're my laughter, my joy, my heartache and my soul mate. Without you I'm an empty vessel, but with you I truly live.'

From the moment Jack had seen Sophie on the veranda he'd lurched from wanting to hate her to wanting to pull her into his arms and never let her go. His previous fear for Imogen had unravelled him to the point of incoherency—to have lost them both would have killed him. Now he gazed down into Sophie's tear-stained face and saw the truth in her eyes, heard it in her voice; his hurt faded and his battered heart healed. She really did love him and Im.

He pulled her towards him and buried his face in her hair. 'God, Sophie, I thought I'd lost both of you.'

Her arms wrapped around his waist, her head on his chest. 'Then you totally understand how I've been feeling.'

He tilted her chin up with his fingers so he could see her face. 'I so do. Are you absolutely certain you want to make a family and live the life of an Armitage? Because I can't go through the last two days ever again.'

'I'm so sorry I put us through this, Jack. I love you. I love everything about you—even the lists.'

He instantly relaxed. 'You really do love me.'

Her eyes shone and she smiled. 'I really do love you, and seeing I'm down on my knees it seems appropriate that I ask you a question.'

He grinned. 'Is that why you're down there?'

She laughed and playfully slapped his thigh. 'Jack Armitage, will you make me the happiest woman in the world by making an honest woman of me, living with me in Barragong and helping me raise our children?'

Joy flooded him and he pulled her to her feet before rolling her onto the bed and kissing her thoroughly. Now he was truly home.

Sophie gave herself up to his kiss, loving the feel of his body pressing against her and his mouth roving over her lips, but as his hand touched her breast she gave him a gentle push, breaking the kiss. 'We're in your mother's bedroom.'

He laughed a wicked chuckle. 'I never thought I'd find your sexual-embarrassment button.'

She gave him a sheepish smile. 'I really want to have a good relationship with your mother, but acting like a total tart in her bedroom on the first day I meet her might jeopardise things.'

He trailed a finger down her cheek. 'She's going to love you. She'll be in seventh heaven, because this Christmas she's getting a new daughter and a granddaughter.' He stood up and pulled her with him. 'Come on, let's go and tell everyone the good news.'

'Can I at least splash my face? I must look a fright.'

He cupped her cheeks. 'You're beautiful, Sophie. I

think I've loved you from the moment you and your backpack walked in the hospital.'

She laid her head on his shoulder, in awe that she'd found this man so full of love, care and delicious sexuality, and he that he loved her back. 'You had me weak at the knees with your bad-boy persona, but I fell in love with all of you.'

'So if things ever get a bit stale all I need to do is take us for a ride on the bike?'

She grinned. 'That will do it every time.' But her smile faded because she knew there was one more thing she had to ask. 'Jack, I know you say your trip is no longer necessary, but are you absolutely certain you have no regrets?'

He tucked a stray curl behind her ear. 'We'll get a locum and you, Imogen and I will take a three-month holiday. We'll camp under the stars at Uluru, feed the dolphins at Monkey Mia and swim in the crystal waters of Jim Jim Falls, and by the time we get back you'll be a fair-dinkim Aussie.'

'That sounds perfect to me.'

Santa came to Barragong on the CFS fire truck, his suit as red and rosy as the vehicle. His jolly belly wobbled, and his violet eyes sparkled as he handed out lollies and listened to the children's gift requests.

Imogen held Sophie's hand as she waited her turn. 'Did Jack have to go to the hospital?'

Sophie nodded, wondering if she'd be struck down for the half-truth. Jack had gone to the hospital to get changed into the Santa costume. She wondered if all the padding and the white whiskers were enough to fox her very intelligent daughter. 'He'll be here for your concert.'

'Great to see you here, Sophie.' A proud and smiling Max passed by, cuddling his new daughter.

Elsie Stephenson, her arm linked through her husband's, gave her a wave. 'You did a great job on that costume, Sophie.'

Sophie smiled and waved, pinching herself at the fact that this was her town and these were her people.

Christmas Eve in Barragong was a community event and everyone in the district was there. The aroma of onions floated through the air as the Rotary Club cooked up a score of sausages and hamburgers for the hungry crowd. The stage was the flat bed of a huge Mack truck; the primary-school choir sang *Six White Boomers* and *Rudolph*, and the high-school band had done a stunning version of *Joy To The World*. The talented young soloist had reduced Sophie to tears with *When a Child Is Born*.

Imogen had held her hand and said, 'Christmas is happy, Sophie.'

Jack had hugged her, saying, 'It's in our future.'

'Who's next?' Santa's deep voice boomed.

'It's my turn!' Imogen ran up to Santa and sat on his lap.

Sophie took a photo; the moment she got home, she'd upload it and email it to her father. Jack had insisted she ring him as soon as they'd had a celebratory glass of champagne with his family. She'd spoken to her dad and each of her sisters, and Minty had said, 'I'm so glad for you, sis. Dad was starting to worry I'd put you off kids, but I told him you weren't that silly!'

Then Jack had seized the phone and spent ten minutes talking to her father. When he'd hung up, he'd said, 'He sounds like a good bloke and I invited him for next Christmas.'

She loved the idea of that.

Min wandered over, tanned and healthy from her cruise and a lovely smile on her face. 'I loved my Pacific holiday, but there's nothing like a Barragong Christmas.' She passed Sophie a glass of wine and then raised her glass. 'I've wanted Jack to find this sort of happiness for a very long time, so thank you.'

Sophie felt the tears hovering again. 'I broke his heart.'

Min's nodded. 'But you mended it, and that's all that matters.'

Imogen ran back to them holding a lolly on a stick. 'Look what Santa gave me.'

Min smiled. 'I can mind that for you, because I can see your kinder teacher getting all the kids to line up for the concert.'

Imogen's eyes sparkled. 'Is it time for me to be an emu?'

'It's time.'

Ten minutes later, Sophie felt an arm snake around her waist. 'How did it go?'

Jack grinned. 'She never suspected a thing.' He grabbed her hand. 'Come on, shake a leg and hustle; we need to be at the front to take photos of our daughter's very first concert.'

The music started and the children came on dressed as kangaroos, wombats, emus, bilbies and possums. They gathered around the manger and baby Caitlyn was a true professional—she slept through the entire play. Imogen, as the emu innkeeper, carried her tray and said in a loud voice, 'We are full, but you can sleep in the stable.'

Sophie thought her heart would burst with pride.

As the nativity play ended, the evening star rose high

in the sky and everyone lit their candles and joined together to sing the Aussie version of *Jingle Bells*.

Min held Imogen in her arms and Im carefully held her candle, gripping it in the plastic holder, while singing lustily and off-key.

Sophie leaned back against Jack, whose arms wrapped tightly around her.

He whispered in her ear, 'Do you miss the cold and the snow?'

'Not at all. I love all these new Christmas traditions.'

He grinned like an excited kid. 'I can't wait to give you your present in the morning.'

She turned in his arms and gazed up at him. 'I don't need a present, Jack. You've given me yourself and Imogen, and you've given me back Christmas. I'm the luckiest and happiest woman alive.'

He hugged her tightly. 'Merry Christmas, my darling Sophie.'

'Merry Christmas, Jack.' And she hugged him right back.

THE MIDWIFE'S CHRISTMAS MIRACLE

by Jennifer Taylor

Midwife Lucy Harris has no trouble believing Dr Max Curtis's playboy reputation! She longs to be immune to his dark good looks, but Max's tenderness towards his tiny patients thaws her frozen heart… As the village's festive lights twinkle, Lucy finds her thoughts turn from medicine…to marriage!

THE DOCTOR'S SOCIETY SWEETHEART

by Lucy Clark

Socialite Emmy is determined to show her boss Dr Dartagnan Freeman that she's more dedicated to triage than tiaras! Before long Dart discovers that Emmy is a warm, compassionate doctor… Could Australia's sweetheart be bringing his heart back to life?

On sale from 3rd December 2010
Don't miss out!

Available at WHSmith, Tesco, ASDA, Eason and all good bookshops
www.millsandboon.co.uk